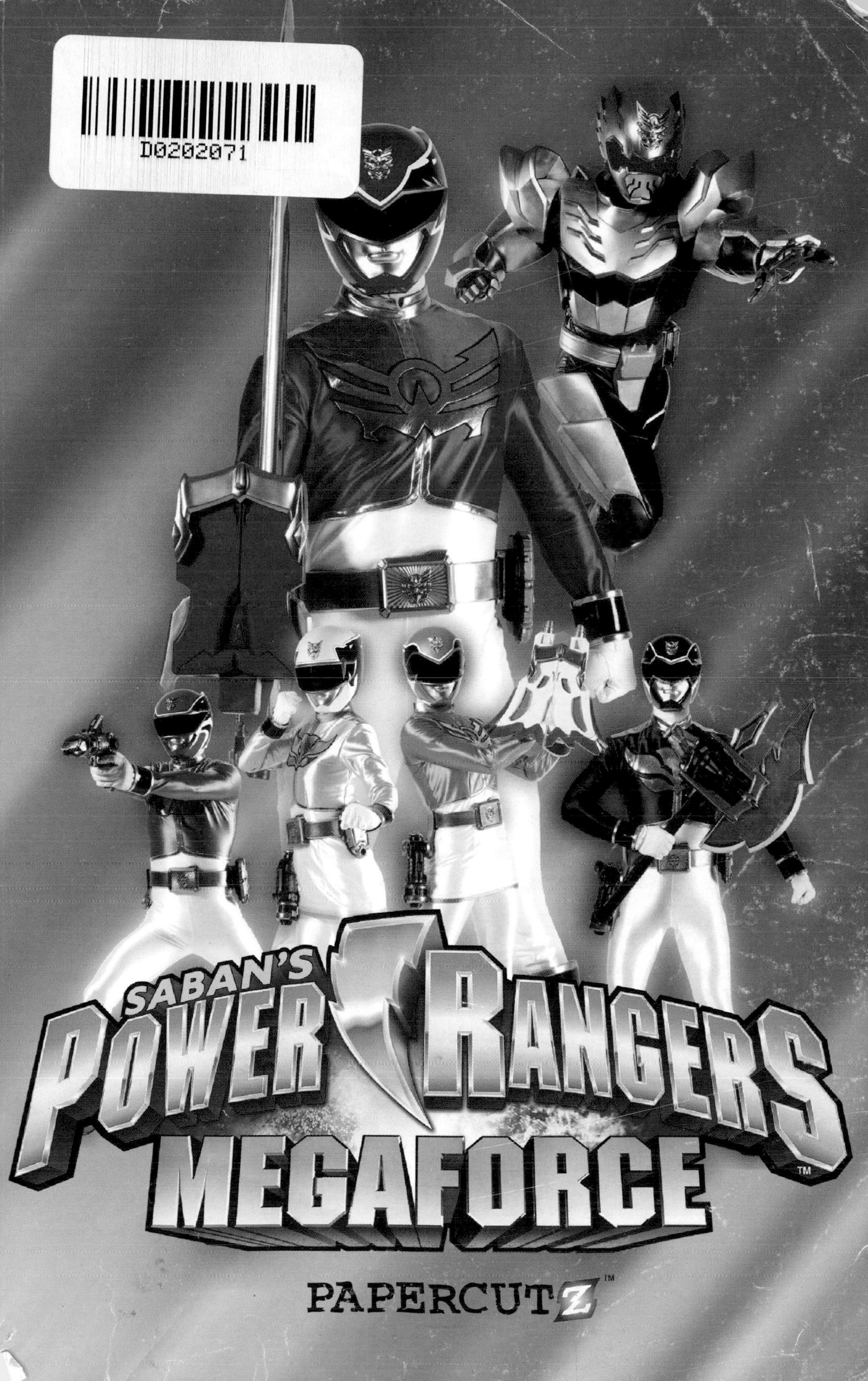
SABAN'S
POWER RANGERS
MEGAFORCE™
PAPERCUTZ™

Graphic Novels Available From PAPERCUTZ™

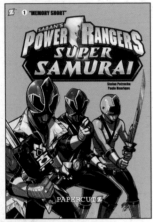

Graphic Novel #1

Graphic Novel #2

Graphic Novel #3

Coming Soon

Graphic Novel #4

**Mighty Morphin Power Rangers
Graphic Novel #1**

SABAN'S POWER RANGERS MEGAFORCE

4 "BROKEN WORLD"

Stefan Petrucha – Writer

PH Marcondes – Artist

Laurie E. Smith– Colorist

PAPERCUTZ™
New York

SABAN'S POWER RANGERS MEGAFORCE
#4 "BROKEN WORLD"

STEFAN PETRUCHA -- Writer
PH MARCONDES -- Artist
LAURIE E. SMITH -- Colorist
BRYAN SENKA -- Letterer

UMESH PATEL (RANGER CREW) -- Special Thanks
KAY OLIVER & MARY RAFFERTY -- Extra Special Thanks
DAWN K. GUZZO -- Production
BETH SCORZATO -- Production Coordinator
MICHAEL PETRANEK -- Editor
JIM SALICRUP
Editor-in-Chief

ISBN: 978-1-59707-392-9 paperback edition
ISBN: 978-1-59707-393-6 hardcover edition

Printed in China
December 2013 by New Era Printing LTD.
Unit C. 8/F Worldwide Centre
123 Chung Tau, Kowloon
Hong Kong

Papercutz books may be purchased for business or promotional use. For information on bulk purchases please contact
Macmillan Corporate and Premium Sales Department at (800) 221-7945 x5442.

Distributed by Macmillan

First Printing

MEET SABAN'S POWER RANGERS MEGAFORCE

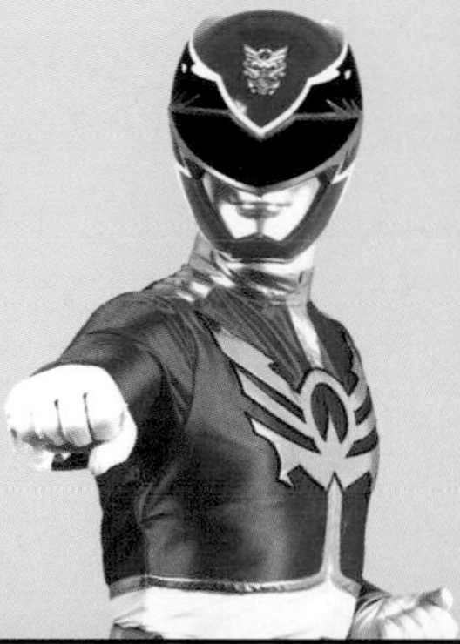

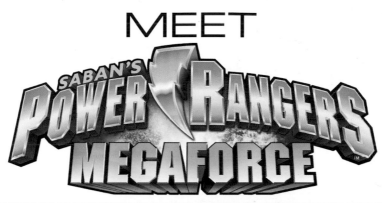

For centuries, the Earth has been protected by a supernatural guardian being named Gosei and his robotic aide, Tensou. When the evil Warstar aliens begin their massive invasion, Gosei calls upon five teenagers to form the ultimate team...
the Power Rangers Megaforce!

Using their newfound abilities, mega-weapons, tech Zords and Megazords, the fate of the world rests in the hands of the Power Rangers Megaforce.

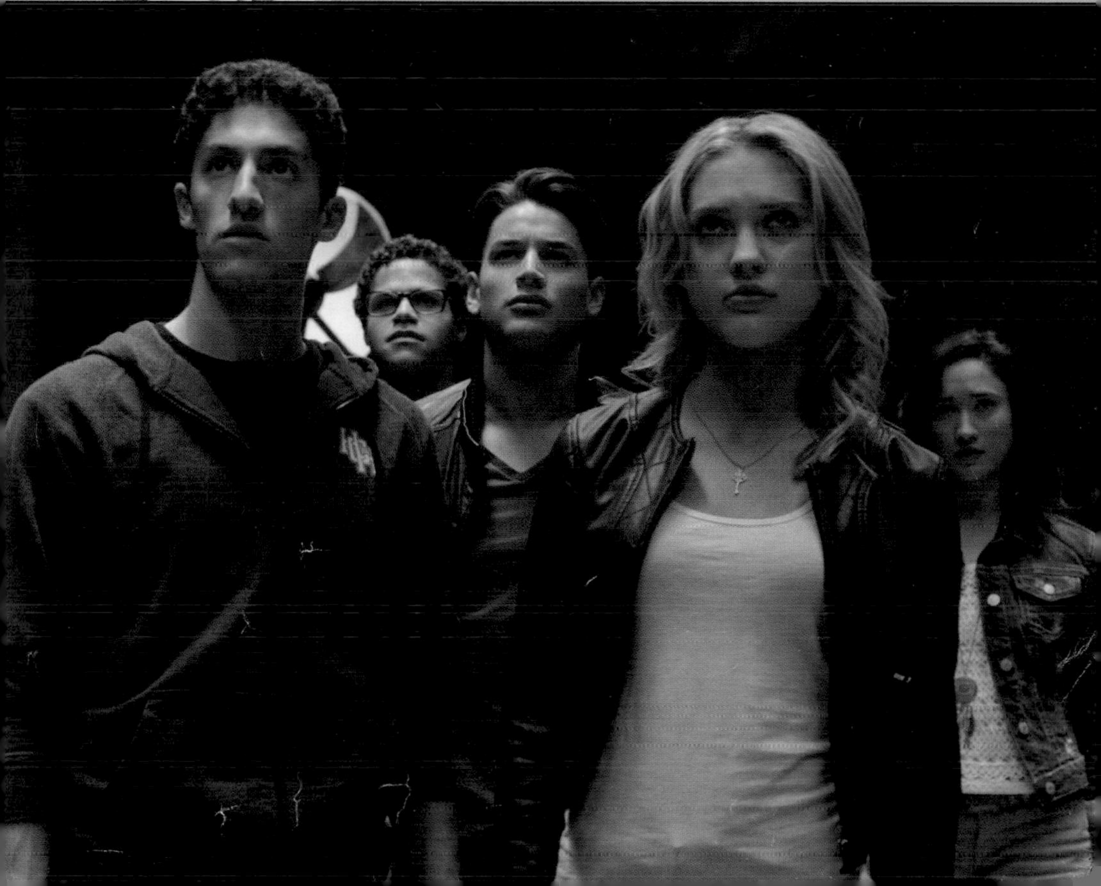

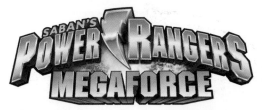

THE RED RANGER (TROY BURROWS)

Troy finds himself as the new kid in town... again. Moving often has made Troy grow up fast, as he had to quickly learn how to take care of himself. Troy is a bit of a loner, but he's eager to make friends in his new hometown. His life, however, is about to take an unexpected turn.

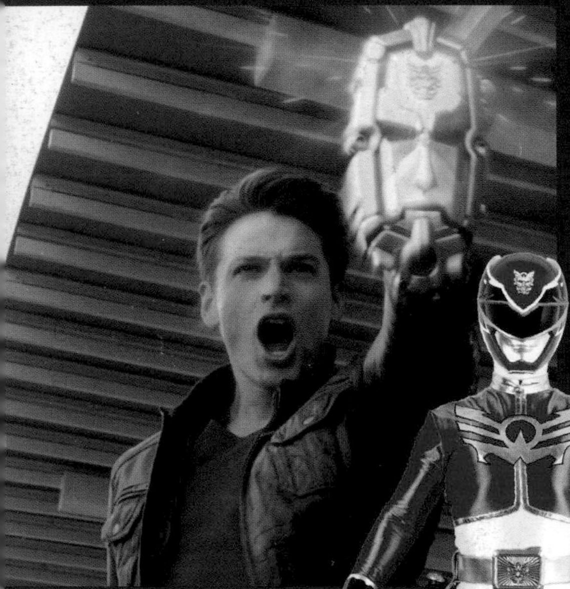

Troy enjoys practicing and perfecting his martial arts skills. He's got the focus and discipline to make him a force to be reckoned with. He doesn't look for trouble but he'll never run from it when someone is in need. Compassionate and loyal, Troy is a champion of the underdog be they human or alien.

As the series begins, Troy is grateful when he makes friends with the other teens and is united with them as the Megaforce. Troy never expected to be the leader of the Megaforce, but with his manner, discipline, and karate skills, it's as if he were training for the job all his life. A natural leader, he quickly rises to the challenge of becoming the newest Red Ranger and leading his comrades into every skirmish with courage and determination.

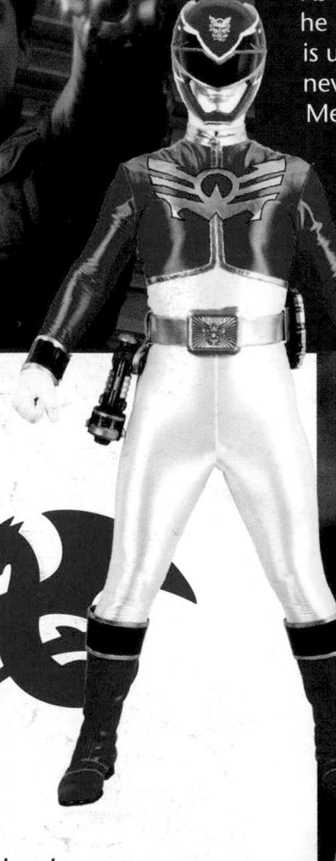

Weapon:
Dragon Sword

Elemental Power:
Sky

Zord:
Dragon

Signature Move:
Sky Dragon

Notes:
It's his destiny to lead the Megaforce.

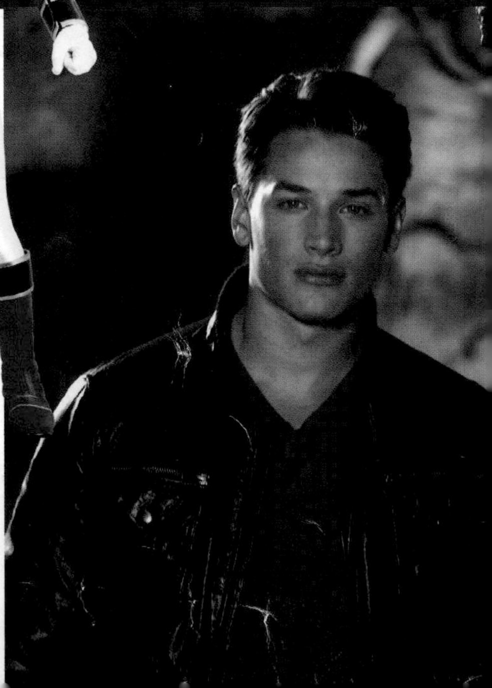

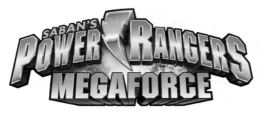

SABAN'S POWER RANGERS MEGAFORCE

THE PINK RANGER (EMMA GOODALL)

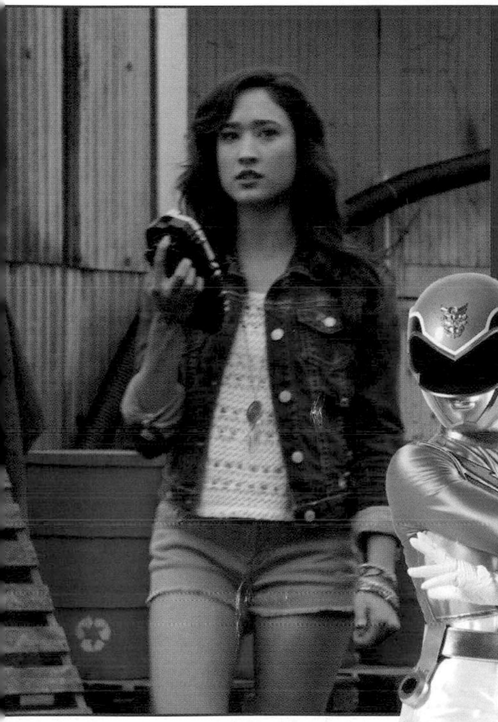

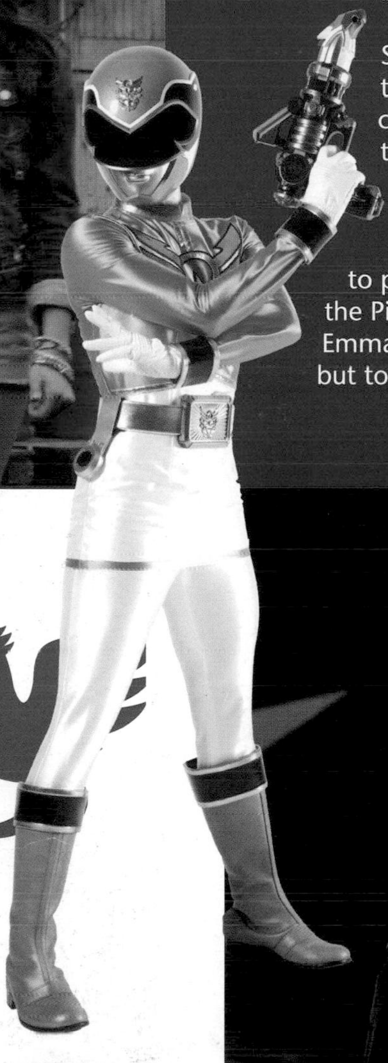

Emma is a compassionate and charitable teen who will do what it takes to protect the environment. While photography is a great way for Emma to express her love of nature, her more wild side has a desire to be a BMX biker.

Surprised like the rest of the Ranger team when called upon to be part of the Megaforce, Emma takes the alien attacks on the environment personally and is anxious to protect the world. As the Pink Ranger, not only is it Emma's goal to save the world, but to make it a better place.

Weapon:
Phoenix Flare

Elemental Power:
Sky

Zord:
Phoenix

Signature Move:
Air Phoenix

Notes:
Emma is a skilled BMX cyclist.

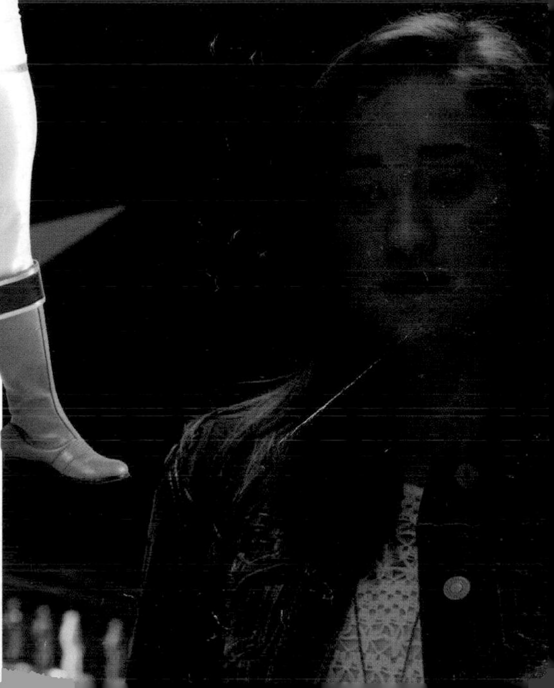

SABAN'S POWER RANGERS MEGAFORCE

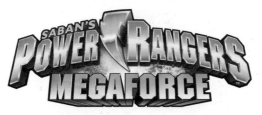

THE BLUE RANGER (NOAH CARVER)

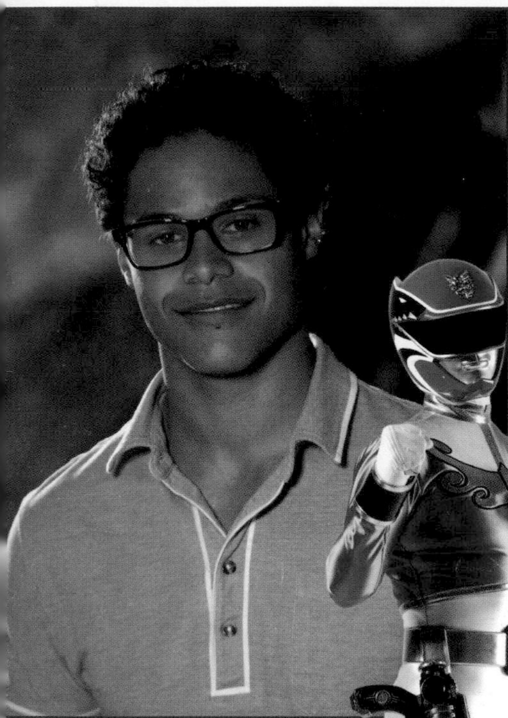

The school's geek, Noah is incredibly clever and kind, but a bit socially akward. He often finds himself dragged into social adventures by Jake, the Black Ranger, when he would rather remain safely in the warm glow of a computer monitor. He has an insatiable thirst for knowledge and is awed by the fact that aliens are attacking the Earth. Since becoming a Ranger, he is even more excited by the technology that the team gets to use in their battles.

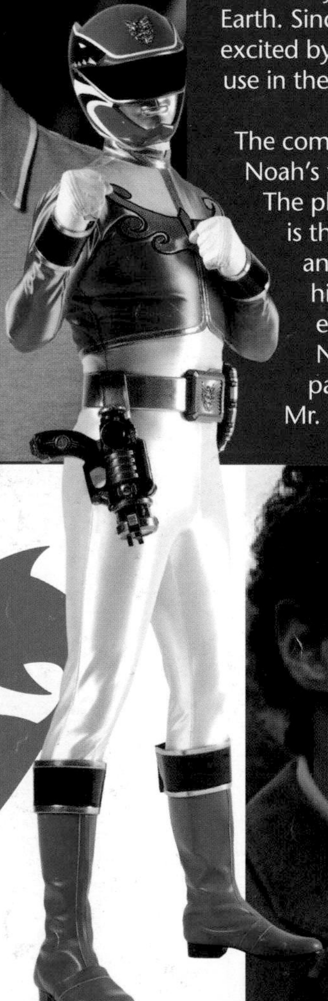

The combination of Jake's social savvy and Noah's tech skills make them a great team. The physical part of being a Power Ranger is the hardest part for Noah but with Troy and Jake being at his side, they encourage him to try. In the end, Noah succeeds by employing his true strength-- brainpower. Noah shares his love of science and the paranormal with his goofy science teacher, Mr. Burley.

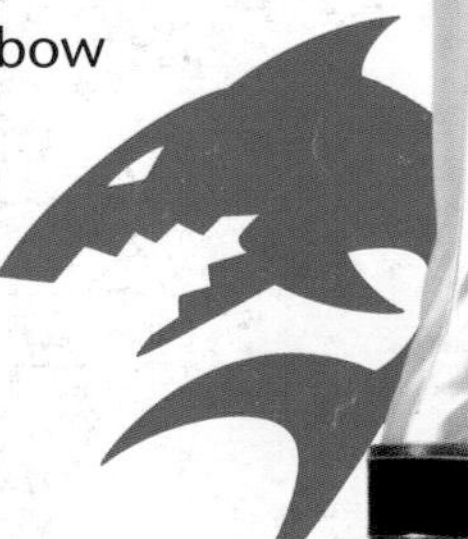

Weapon:
Shark bow

Element:
Sea

Zord:
Shark

Notes:
Noah shares his love of the paranormal with his science teacher, Mr. Burley.

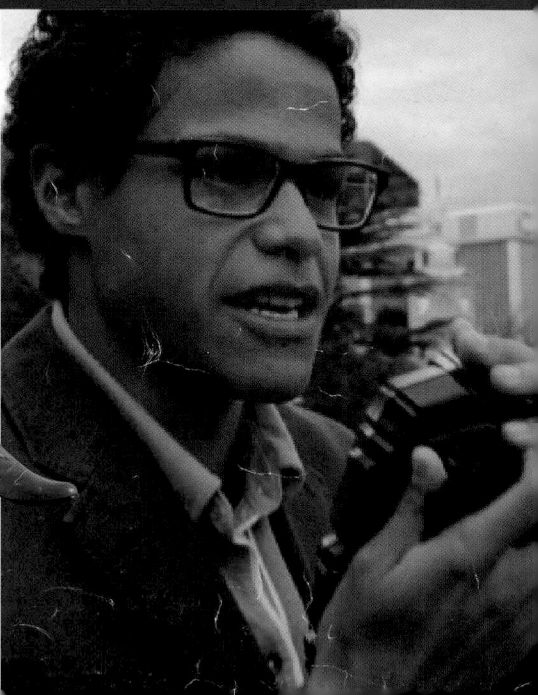

SABAN'S POWER RANGERS MEGAFORCE

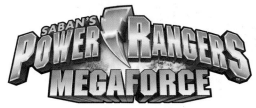

THE YELLOW RANGER (GIA MORAN)

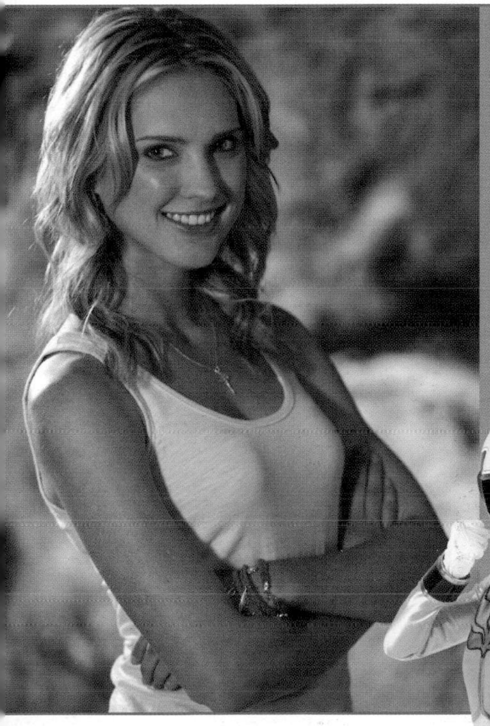

Gia is beautiful, smart and a formidable martial artist with a generally unflappable demeanor. Not only is she the prettiest and most intelligent girl at school, she is also the toughest. While her personable manner tempts many boys, her martial art skills keep them at bay. Gia carries herself with a sense of confidence that comes from success.

She is loyal to her friends and is best friends with Emma, the Pink Ranger. They have known each other since they were little girls and have remained friends even though they are now very different.

Gia is the perfect addition to the Power Rangers team even though at times her effortless success furstrates her new teammates, but everyone knows they can count on her.

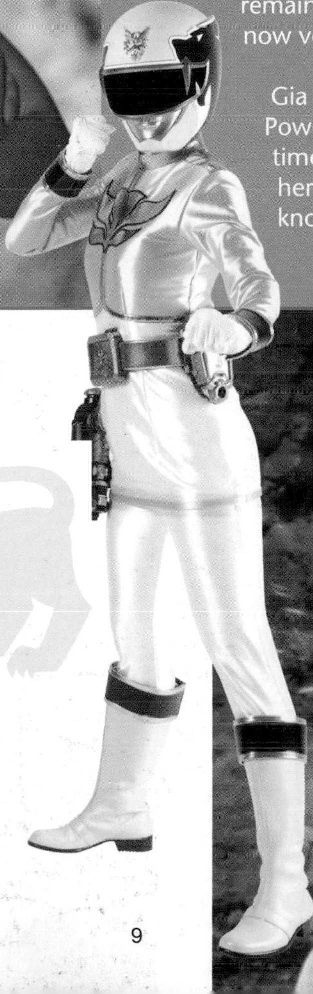

Weapon:
Tiger Claw

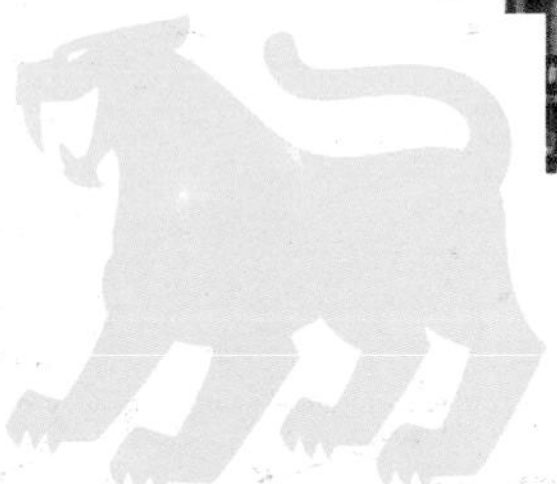

Element:
Earth

Zord:
Tiger

Notes:
Jake (the Black Ranger) has a crush on her.

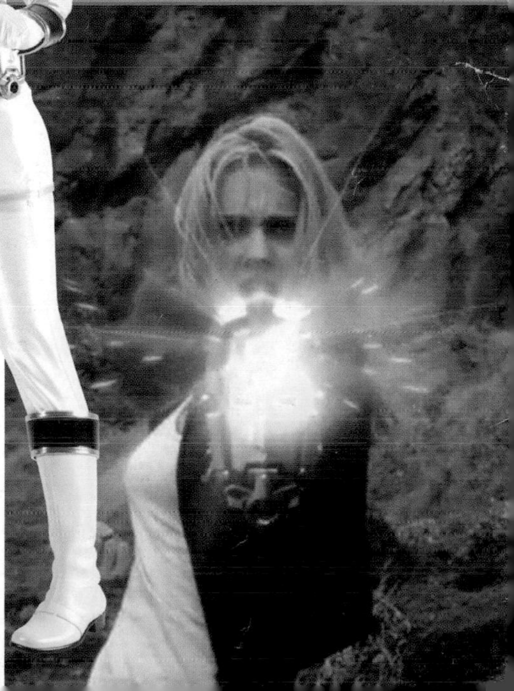

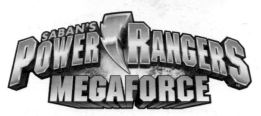

THE BLACK RANGER (JAKE HOLLING)

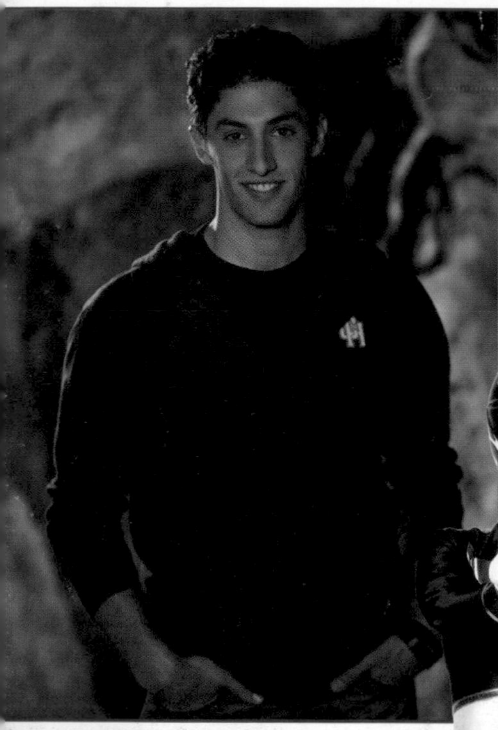

Jake is a fearless, fun-loving teen with a never-ending well of optimism. His athletic abilities are good enough to make the team, but not be the star player. His main passion in life is soccer and it's rare to find him without a soccer ball nearby. Jake's fearlessness also applies to his social life. His determination will not allow something like the lack of an invitation to stop him from going to a party or getting out on the dance floor.

He is best friends with Noah, the Blue Ranger, whom he never stops trying to get to loosen up and have some fun. Jake sees his new super-hero role as an opportunity to do great things even if he occasionally wishes he could let the world know that he's the one saving it. Jake does have one major weak spot and that's his crush on Gia, the Yellow Ranger. He tries to play things cool but he wears his heart on his sleeve and he's certain that one day he'll win her over.

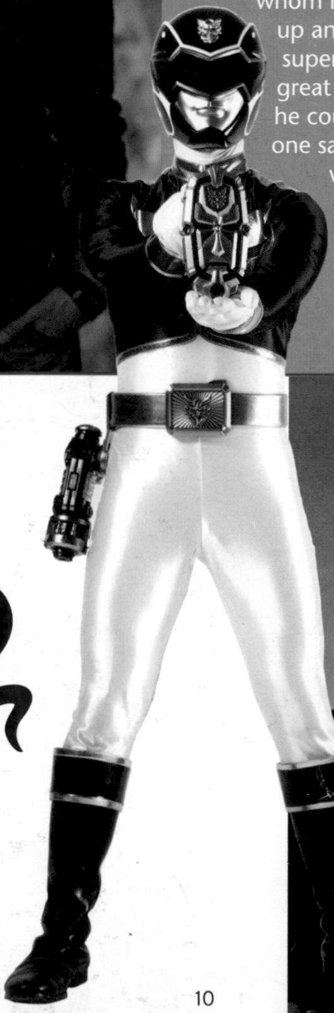

Weapon:
Snake Axe

Elemental Power:
Earth

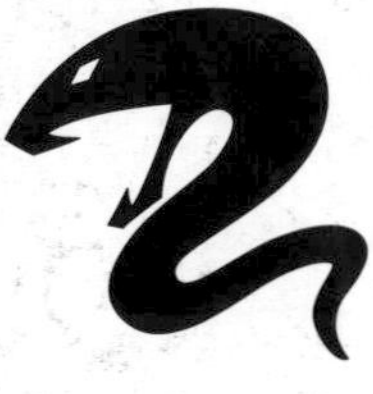

Zord:
Snake

Notes:
Jake is an excellent soccer player, and often has a ball with him.

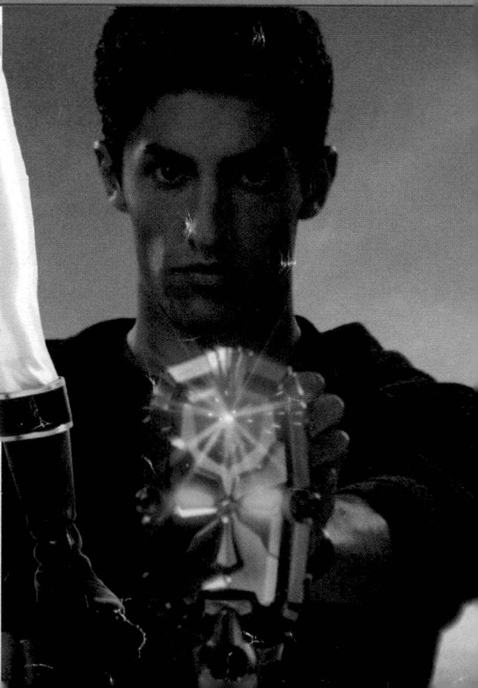

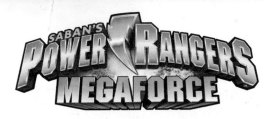

ROBO KNIGHT

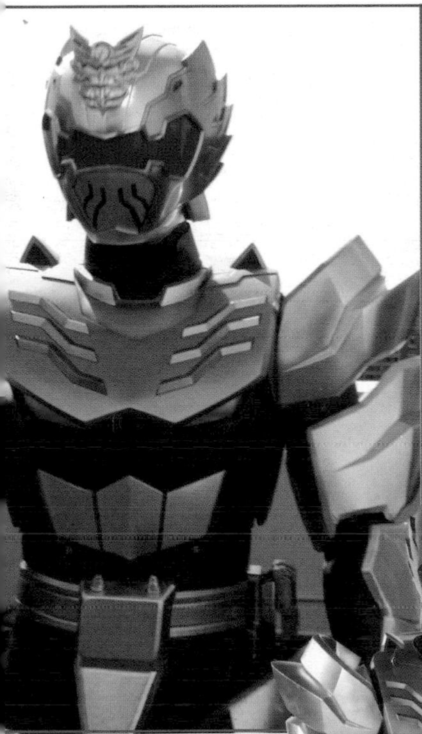

When the Rangers are in the battle for their lives, suddenly there appears an unknown Ranger wearing the same Gosei symbol. The Rangers instantly know he is a part of the Power Rangers. Robo Knight was created by Gosei centuries ago to protect the Earth at all costs. He is powered by the Earth's own elements and he can call on those same elements to use as his powers.

Robo Knight, however, had been buried for centuries and only recently awakened when the Earth sensed danger. The long sleep affected many portions of his memory and now there are times he sees humans as the greatest threat to the Earth. The Power Rangers slowly remind him that there are great attributes to be human and that the Power Rangers see Robo Knight as a good friend-- something he had long forgotten. Unlike the Rangers who have to call their Zords, Robo Knight has the unique ability to morph into his Lion Zord and back again to a robot. A power the Rangers witness firsthand.

Robo Knight learns that humanity's fate is intertwined with Earth's and both are worth saving.

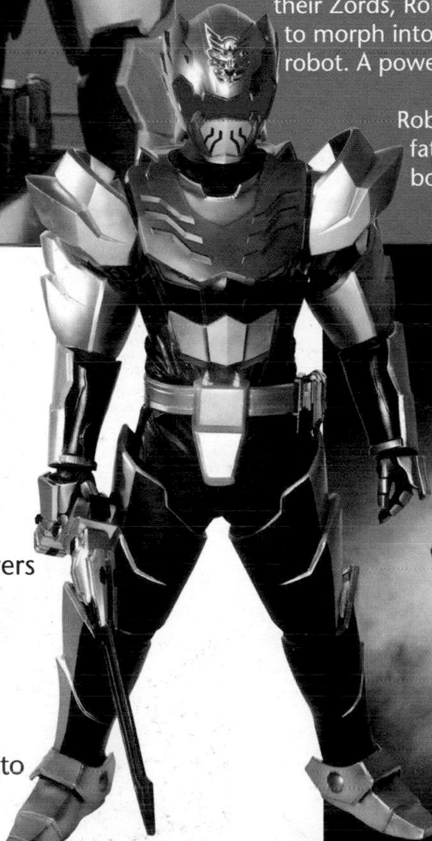

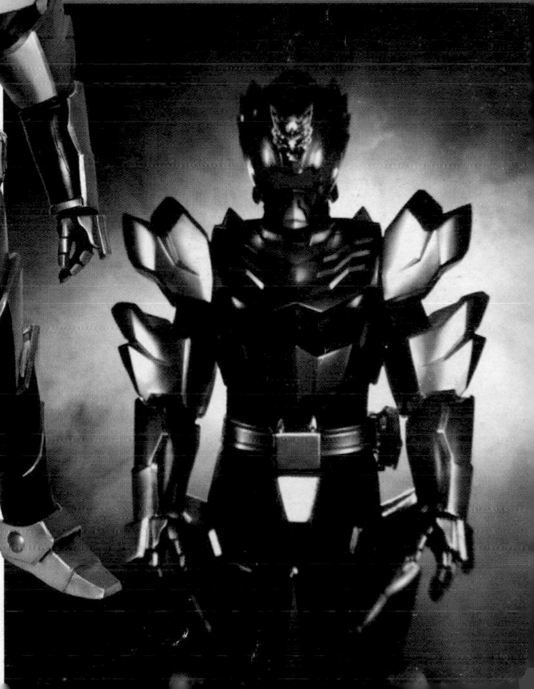

Weapon:
Robo Blaster and Robo Blade

Element:
Access to all Elemental Powers

Zord:
Lion

Notes:
He is the de facto sixth ranger.

SABAN'S POWER RANGERS MEGAFORCE

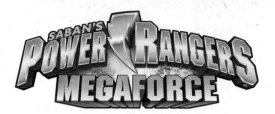

ADMIRAL MALKOR

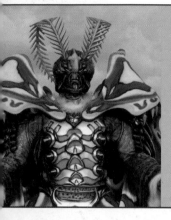

Admiral Malkor is the moth-like commander of the Warstar ship, and the leader of the alien attack force. His goal is to make the Insectoids rule the Earth, and for humans to be nothing but a distant memory. He does not tolerate failure.

VRAK

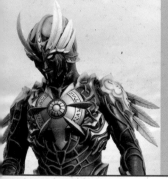

Vrak is not an Insectoid-- he is a member of the alien royal family, and brother to the prince who commands the imminent invasion. He is unique with special powers not possessed by the Insectoids, and seeks to one day use his intelligence to rule over the other aliens, and become emperor.

CREEPOX

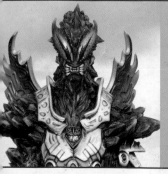

The hulking Insectoid lieutenant that serves at Malkor's side, Creepox, believes firmly in insect superiority. He would like nothing more than to unleash a full-scale attack on planet Earth, and is obsessed with defeating the Red Ranger in one-on-one combat.

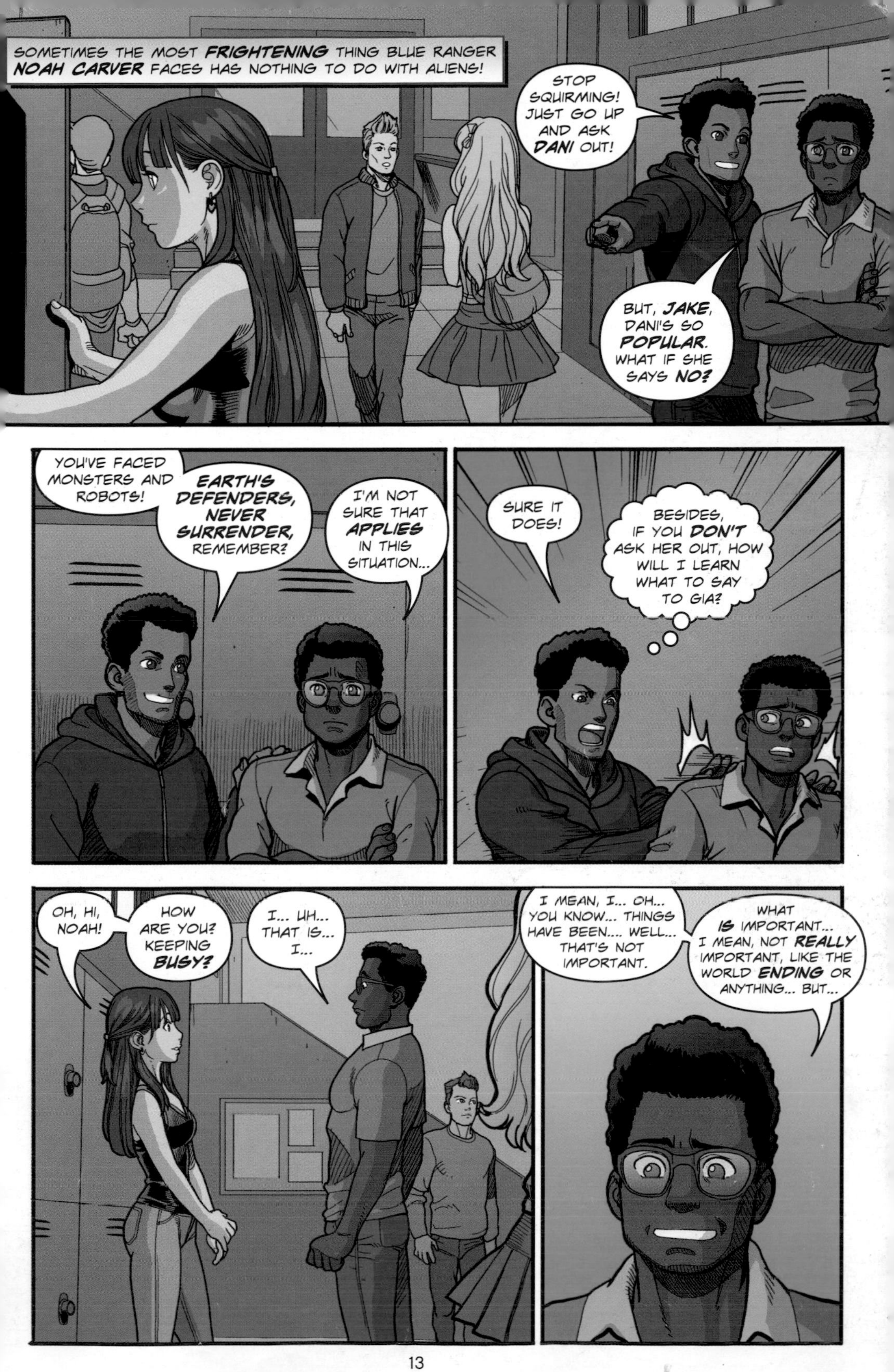

SOMETIMES THE MOST FRIGHTENING THING BLUE RANGER NOAH CARVER FACES HAS NOTHING TO DO WITH ALIENS!
STOP SQUIRMING! JUST GO UP AND ASK DANI OUT!
BUT, JAKE, DANI'S SO POPULAR. WHAT IF SHE SAYS NO?
YOU'VE FACED MONSTERS AND ROBOTS!
EARTH'S DEFENDERS, NEVER SURRENDER, REMEMBER?
I'M NOT SURE THAT APPLIES IN THIS SITUATION...
SURE IT DOES!
BESIDES, IF YOU DON'T ASK HER OUT, HOW WILL I LEARN WHAT TO SAY TO GIA?
OH, HI, NOAH!
HOW ARE YOU? KEEPING BUSY?
I... UH... THAT IS... I...
I MEAN, I... OH... YOU KNOW... THINGS HAVE BEEN.... WELL... THAT'S NOT IMPORTANT.
WHAT IS IMPORTANT... I MEAN, NOT REALLY IMPORTANT, LIKE THE WORLD ENDING OR ANYTHING... BUT...

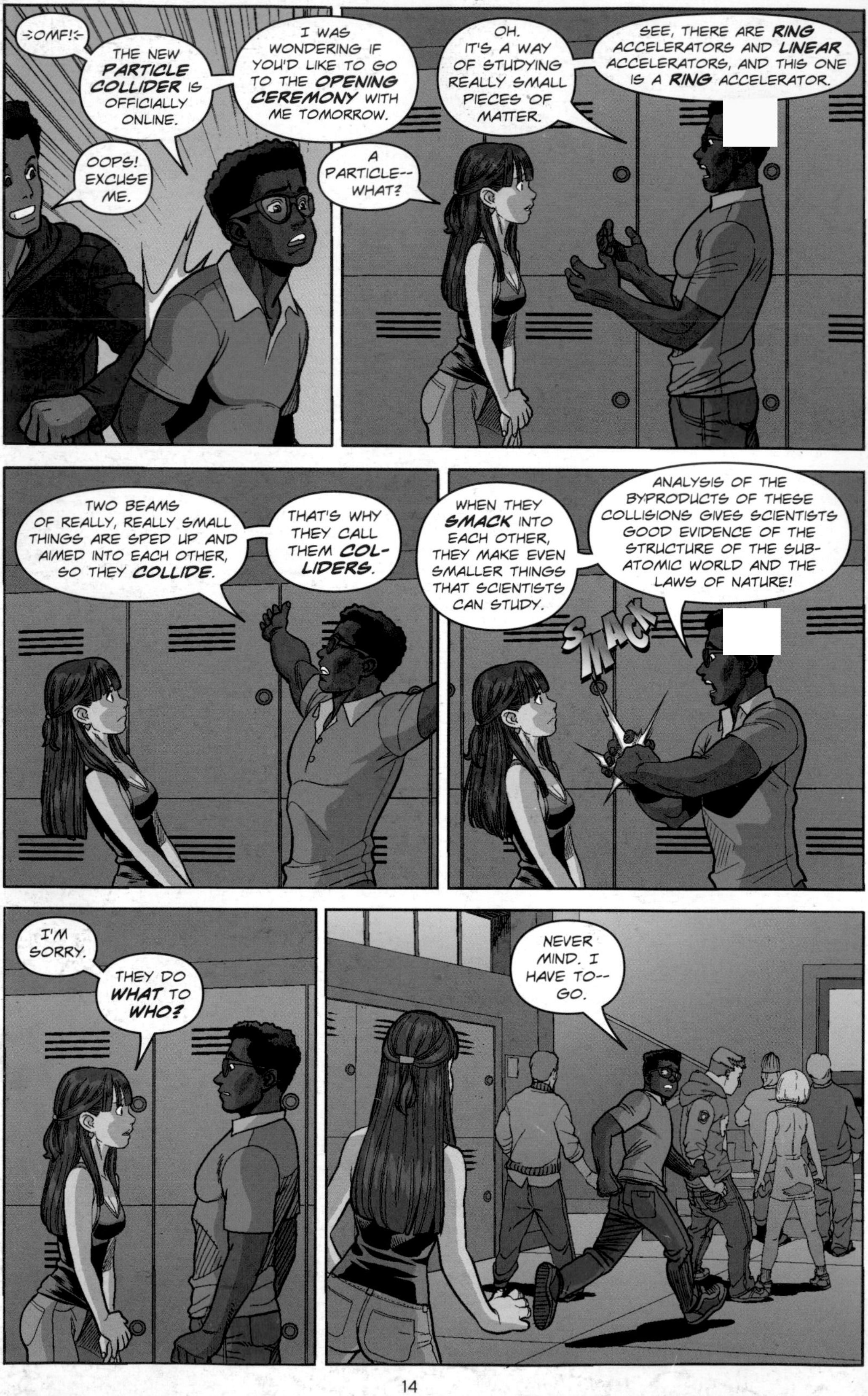

⇒OMF!⇐
THE NEW PARTICLE COLLIDER IS OFFICIALLY ONLINE.
OOPS! EXCUSE ME.
I WAS WONDERING IF YOU'D LIKE TO GO TO THE OPENING CEREMONY WITH ME TOMORROW.
A PARTICLE--WHAT?
OH. IT'S A WAY OF STUDYING REALLY SMALL PIECES OF MATTER.
SEE, THERE ARE RING ACCELERATORS AND LINEAR ACCELERATORS, AND THIS ONE IS A RING ACCELERATOR.
TWO BEAMS OF REALLY, REALLY SMALL THINGS ARE SPED UP AND AIMED INTO EACH OTHER, SO THEY COLLIDE.
THAT'S WHY THEY CALL THEM COL-LIDERS.
WHEN THEY SMACK INTO EACH OTHER, THEY MAKE EVEN SMALLER THINGS THAT SCIENTISTS CAN STUDY.
SMACK
ANALYSIS OF THE BYPRODUCTS OF THESE COLLISIONS GIVES SCIENTISTS GOOD EVIDENCE OF THE STRUCTURE OF THE SUB-ATOMIC WORLD AND THE LAWS OF NATURE!
I'M SORRY.
THEY DO WHAT TO WHO?
NEVER MIND. I HAVE TO--GO.

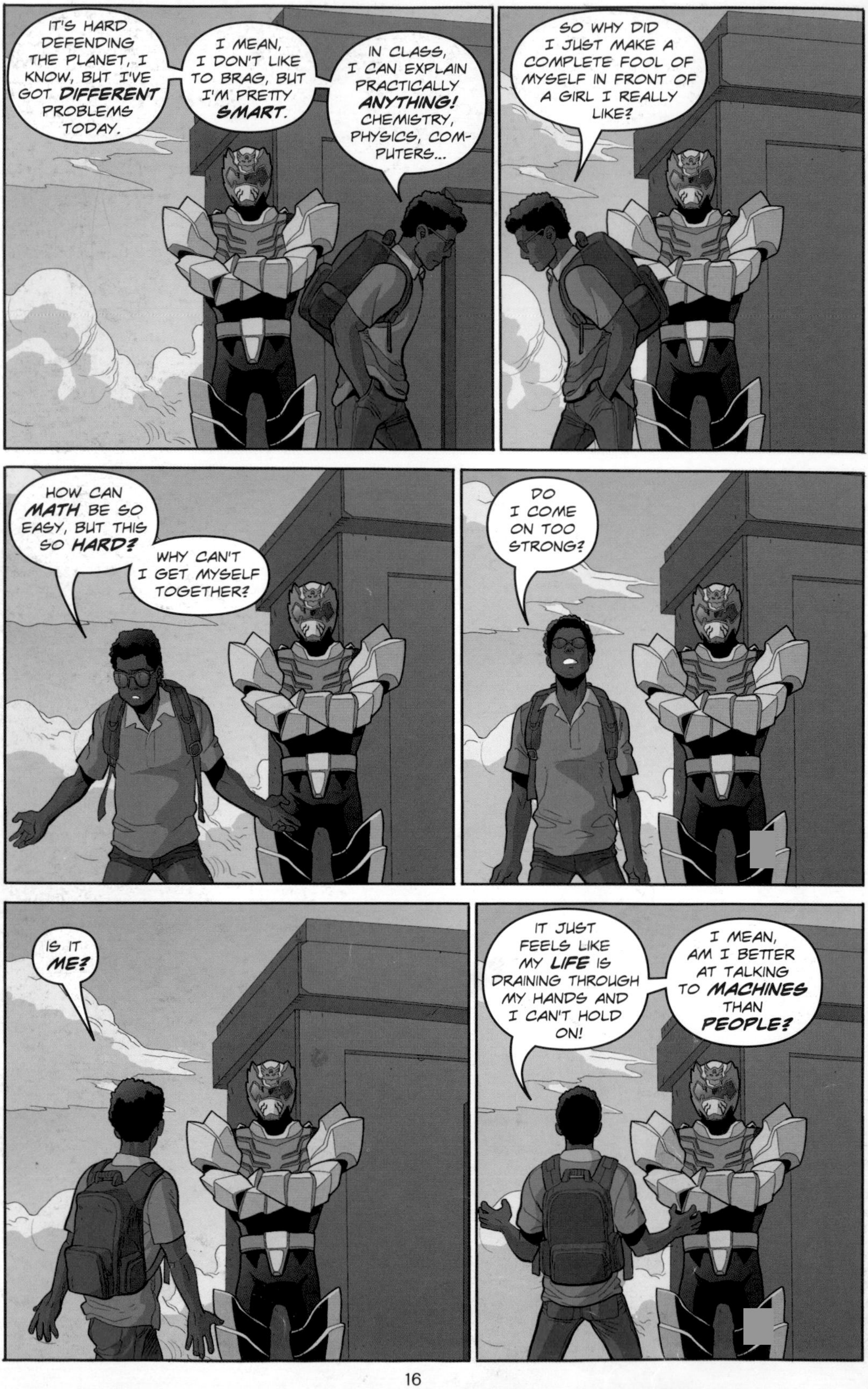

IT'S HARD DEFENDING THE PLANET, I KNOW, BUT I'VE GOT **DIFFERENT** PROBLEMS TODAY.
I MEAN, I DON'T LIKE TO BRAG, BUT I'M PRETTY **SMART**.
IN CLASS, I CAN EXPLAIN PRACTICALLY **ANYTHING!** CHEMISTRY, PHYSICS, COMPUTERS...
SO WHY DID I JUST MAKE A COMPLETE FOOL OF MYSELF IN FRONT OF A GIRL I REALLY LIKE?
HOW CAN **MATH** BE SO EASY, BUT THIS SO **HARD?**
WHY CAN'T I GET MYSELF TOGETHER?
DO I COME ON TOO STRONG?
IS IT **ME?**
IT JUST FEELS LIKE MY **LIFE** IS DRAINING THROUGH MY HANDS AND I CAN'T HOLD ON!
I MEAN, AM I BETTER AT TALKING TO **MACHINES** THAN **PEOPLE?**

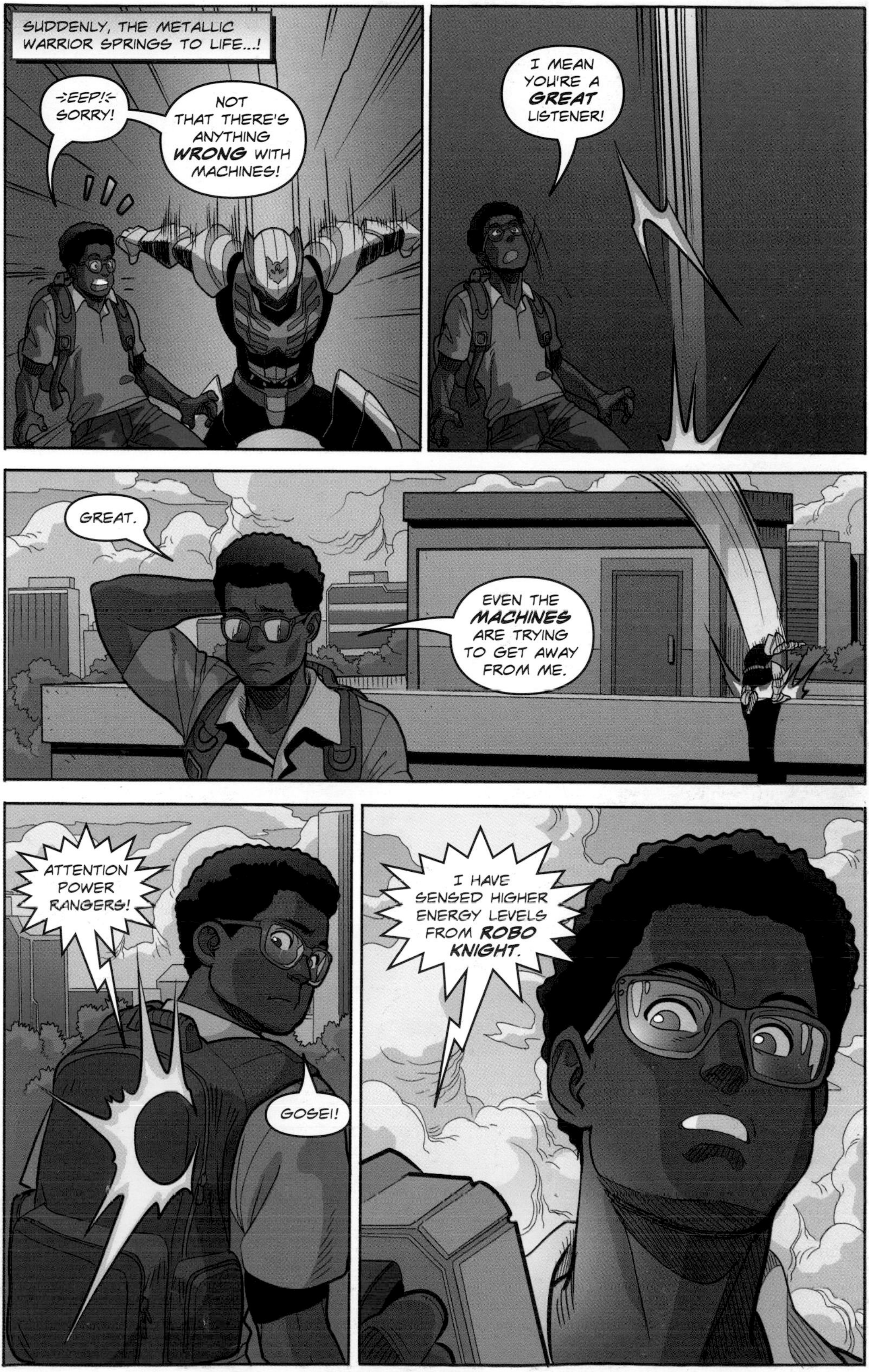
SUDDENLY, THE METALLIC WARRIOR SPRINGS TO LIFE...!
➛EEP!⬸ SORRY!
NOT THAT THERE'S ANYTHING WRONG WITH MACHINES!
I MEAN YOU'RE A GREAT LISTENER!
GREAT.
EVEN THE MACHINES ARE TRYING TO GET AWAY FROM ME.
ATTENTION POWER RANGERS!
GOSEI!
I HAVE SENSED HIGHER ENERGY LEVELS FROM ROBO KNIGHT.

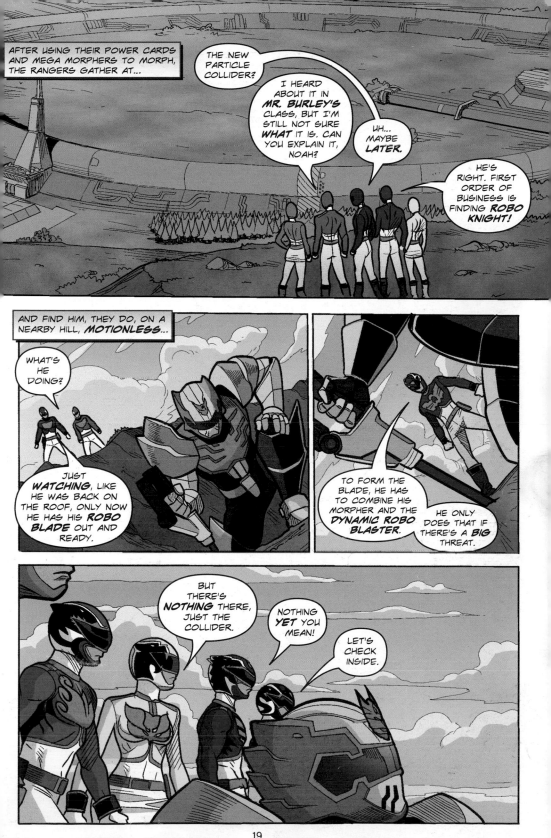

AFTER USING THEIR POWER CARDS AND MEGA MORPHERS TO MORPH, THE RANGERS GATHER AT...

THE NEW PARTICLE COLLIDER?

I HEARD ABOUT IT IN **MR. BURLEY'S** CLASS, BUT I'M STILL NOT SURE **WHAT** IT IS. CAN YOU EXPLAIN IT, NOAH?

UH... MAYBE **LATER.**

HE'S RIGHT. FIRST ORDER OF BUSINESS IS FINDING **ROBO KNIGHT!**

AND FIND HIM, THEY DO, ON A NEARBY HILL, **MOTIONLESS...**

WHAT'S HE DOING?

JUST **WATCHING,** LIKE HE WAS BACK ON THE ROOF, ONLY NOW HE HAS HIS **ROBO BLADE** OUT AND READY.

TO FORM THE BLADE, HE HAS TO COMBINE HIS MORPHER AND THE **DYNAMIC ROBO BLASTER.**

HE ONLY DOES THAT IF THERE'S A **BIG** THREAT.

BUT THERE'S **NOTHING** THERE, JUST THE COLLIDER.

NOTHING **YET** YOU MEAN!

LET'S CHECK INSIDE.

THE POWER RANGERS? HERE?

IS EVERYTHING ALL RIGHT?

THAT'S WHAT WE'RE HERE TO FIND OUT.

YOU'RE ABOUT TO TURN ON THE COLLIDER, RIGHT? COULD SOMETHING GO WRONG?

SOMETHING DANGEROUS?

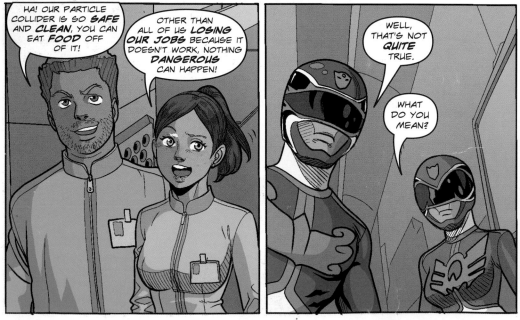

HA! OUR PARTICLE COLLIDER IS SO SAFE AND CLEAN, YOU CAN EAT FOOD OFF OF IT!

OTHER THAN ALL OF US LOSING OUR JOBS BECAUSE IT DOESN'T WORK, NOTHING DANGEROUS CAN HAPPEN!

WELL, THAT'S NOT QUITE TRUE.

WHAT DO YOU MEAN?

20

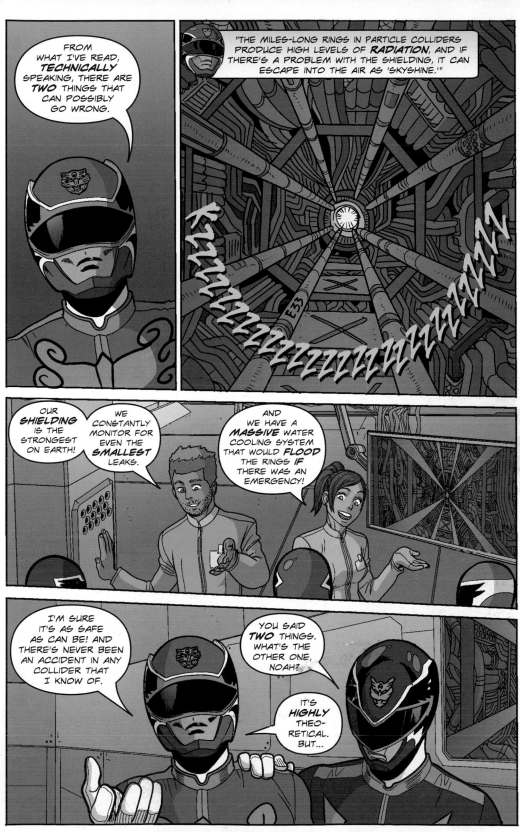

FROM WHAT I'VE READ, *TECHNICALLY* SPEAKING, THERE ARE *TWO* THINGS THAT CAN POSSIBLY GO WRONG.

"THE MILES-LONG RINGS IN PARTICLE COLLIDERS PRODUCE HIGH LEVELS OF *RADIATION*, AND IF THERE'S A PROBLEM WITH THE SHIELDING, IT CAN ESCAPE INTO THE AIR AS 'SKYSHINE.'"

OUR *SHIELDING* IS THE STRONGEST ON EARTH!

WE CONSTANTLY MONITOR FOR EVEN THE *SMALLEST* LEAKS.

AND WE HAVE A *MASSIVE* WATER COOLING SYSTEM THAT WOULD *FLOOD* THE RINGS *IF* THERE WAS AN EMERGENCY!

I'M SURE IT'S AS SAFE AS CAN BE! AND THERE'S NEVER BEEN AN ACCIDENT IN ANY COLLIDER THAT I KNOW OF.

YOU SAID *TWO* THINGS. WHAT'S THE OTHER ONE, NOAH?

IT'S *HIGHLY* THEO-RETICAL. BUT...

21

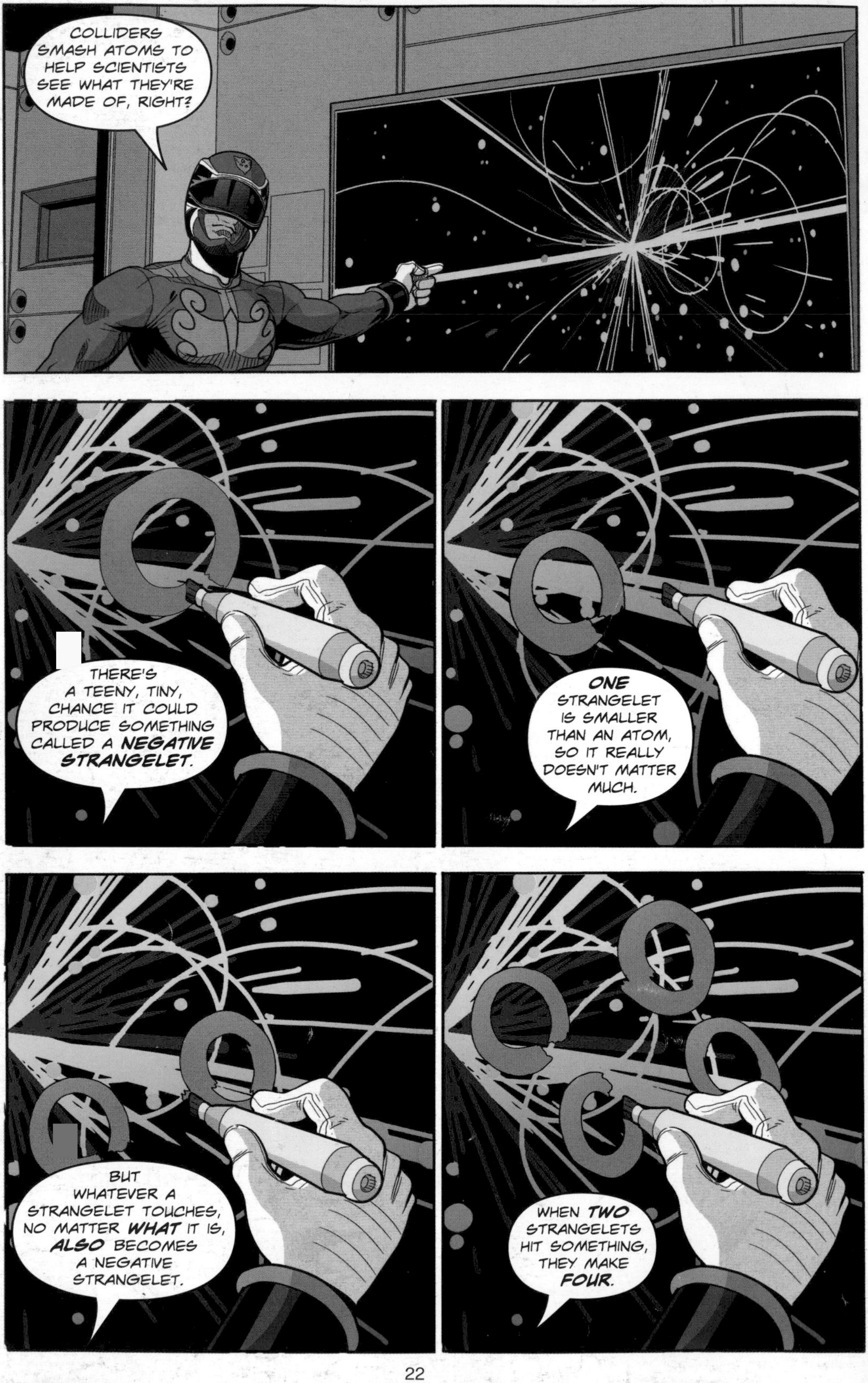
COLLIDERS SMASH ATOMS TO HELP SCIENTISTS SEE WHAT THEY'RE MADE OF, RIGHT?
THERE'S A TEENY, TINY, CHANCE IT COULD PRODUCE SOMETHING CALLED A **NEGATIVE STRANGELET**.
ONE STRANGELET IS SMALLER THAN AN ATOM, SO IT REALLY DOESN'T MATTER MUCH.
BUT WHATEVER A STRANGELET TOUCHES, NO MATTER **WHAT** IT IS, **ALSO** BECOMES A NEGATIVE STRANGELET.
WHEN **TWO** STRANGELETS HIT SOMETHING, THEY MAKE **FOUR**.

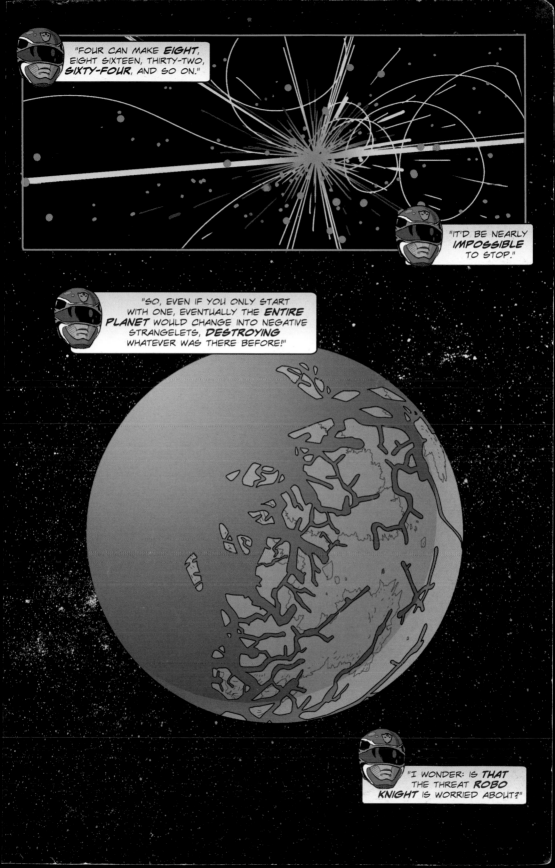

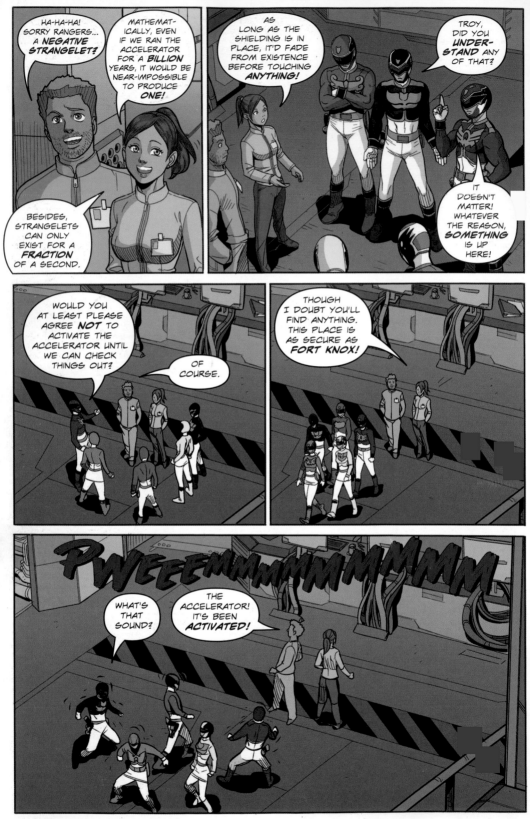

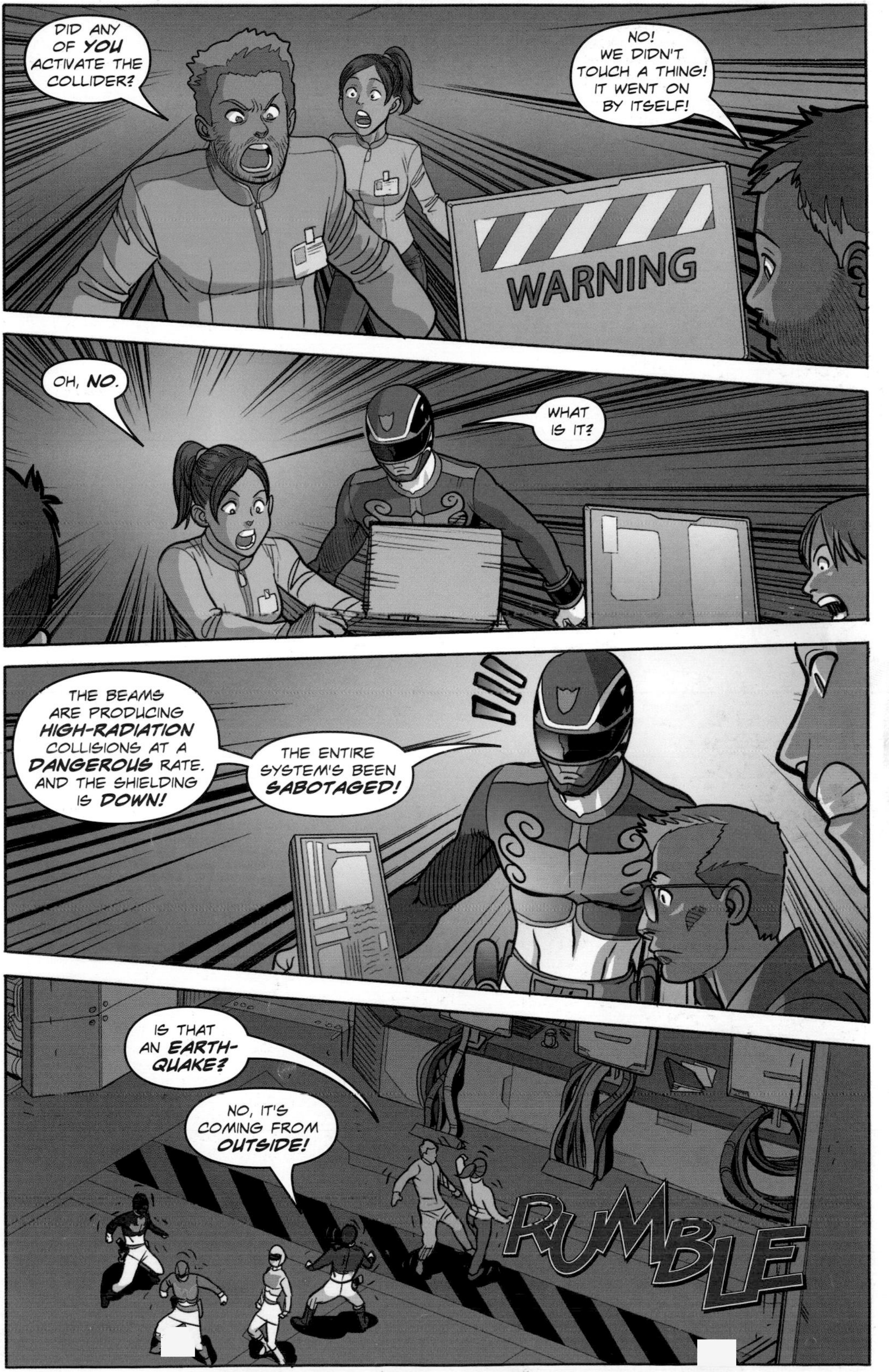
DID ANY OF **YOU** ACTIVATE THE COLLIDER?
NO! WE DIDN'T TOUCH A THING! IT WENT ON BY ITSELF!
WARNING
OH, **NO.**
WHAT IS IT?
THE BEAMS ARE PRODUCING **HIGH-RADIATION** COLLISIONS AT A **DANGEROUS** RATE. AND THE SHIELDING IS **DOWN!**
THE ENTIRE SYSTEM'S BEEN **SABOTAGED!**
IS THAT AN **EARTH-QUAKE?**
NO, IT'S COMING FROM **OUTSIDE!**
RUMBLE

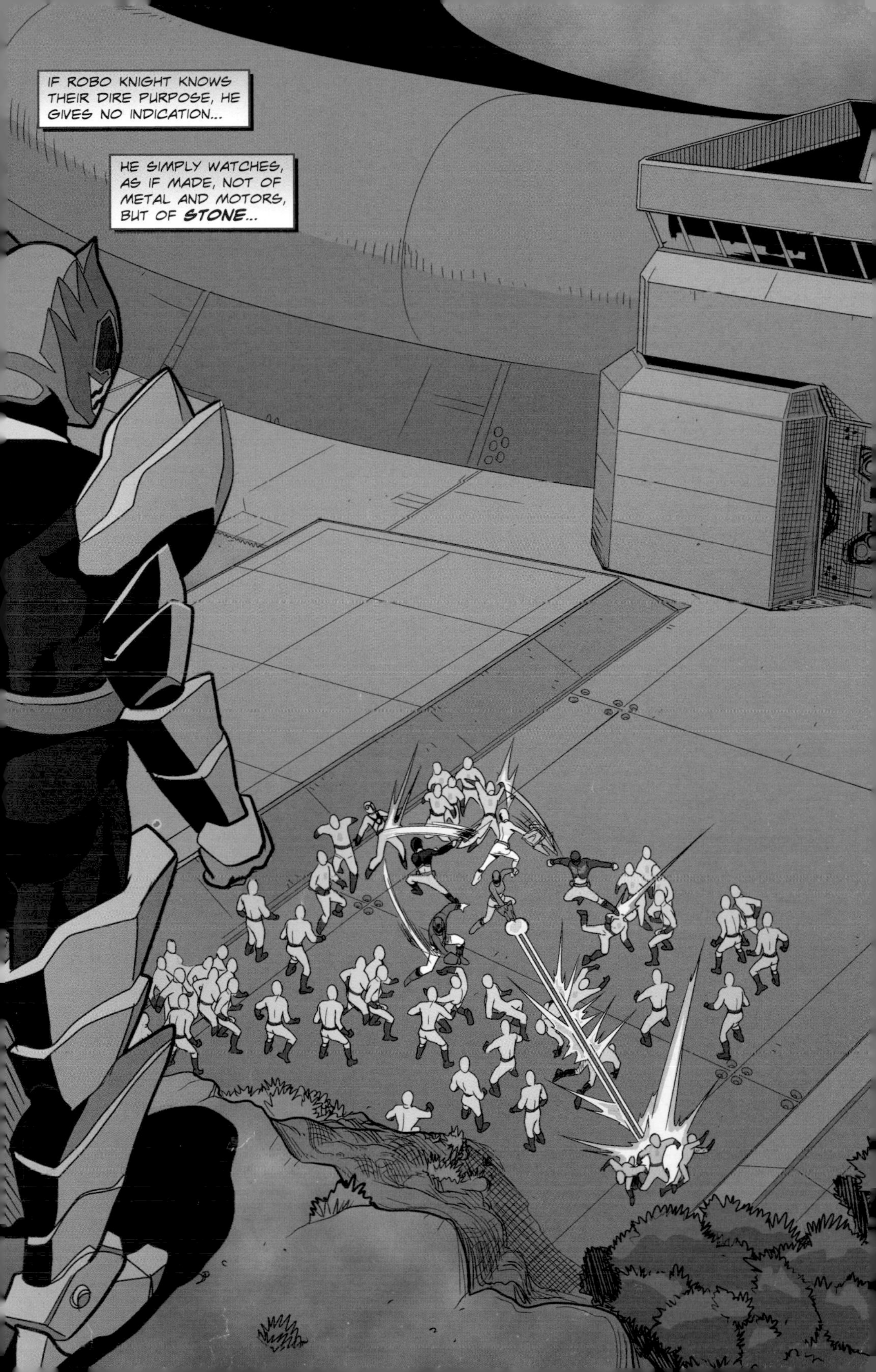
IF ROBO KNIGHT KNOWS THEIR DIRE PURPOSE, HE GIVES NO INDICATION...
HE SIMPLY WATCHES, AS IF MADE, NOT OF METAL AND MOTORS, BUT OF STONE...

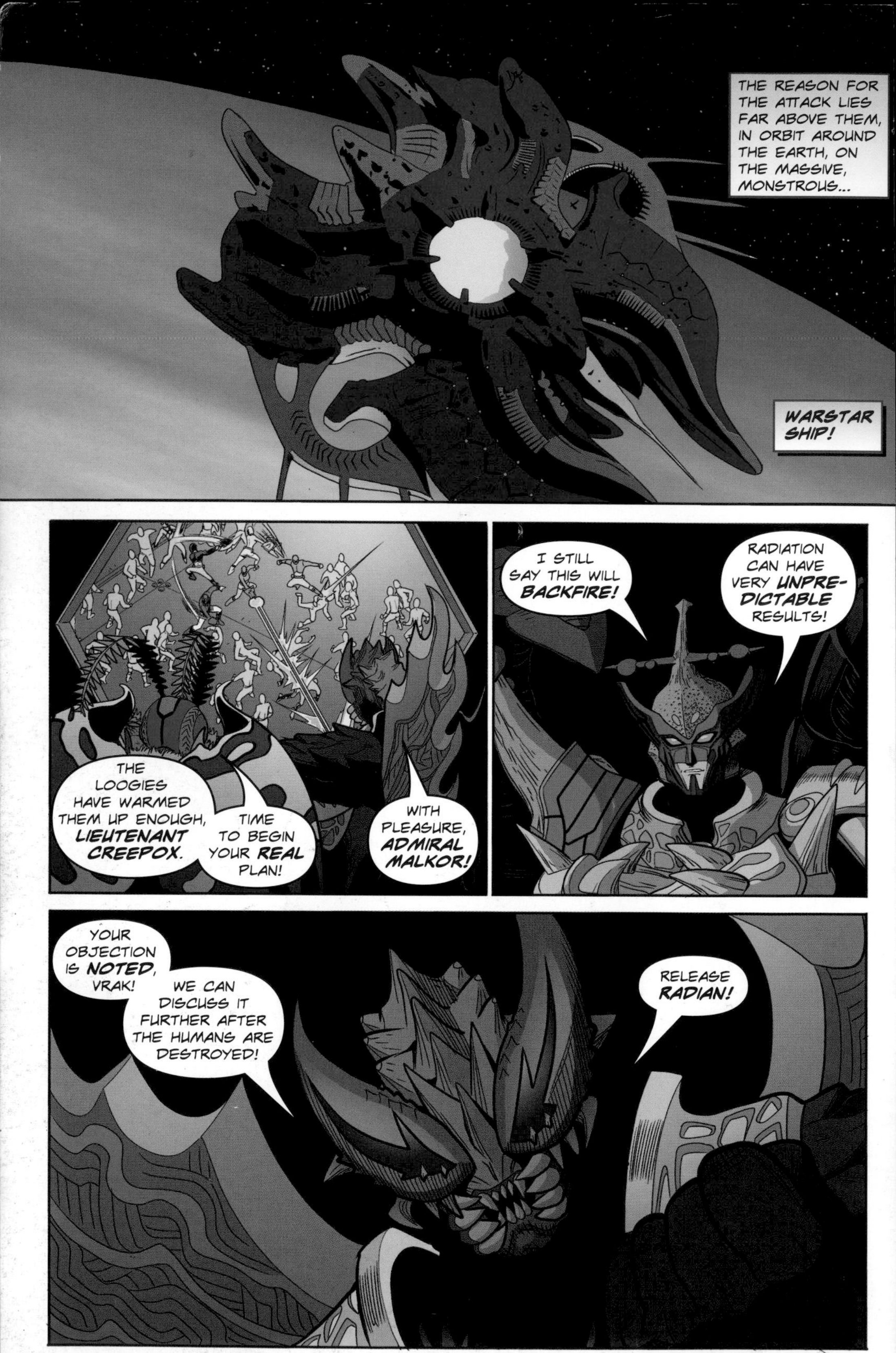
THE REASON FOR THE ATTACK LIES FAR ABOVE THEM, IN ORBIT AROUND THE EARTH, ON THE MASSIVE, MONSTROUS...
WARSTAR SHIP!
THE LOOGIES HAVE WARMED THEM UP ENOUGH, LIEUTENANT CREEPOX.
TIME TO BEGIN YOUR REAL PLAN!
WITH PLEASURE, ADMIRAL MALKOR!
I STILL SAY THIS WILL BACKFIRE!
RADIATION CAN HAVE VERY UNPRE-DICTABLE RESULTS!
YOUR OBJECTION IS NOTED, VRAK!
WE CAN DISCUSS IT FURTHER AFTER THE HUMANS ARE DESTROYED!
RELEASE RADIAN!

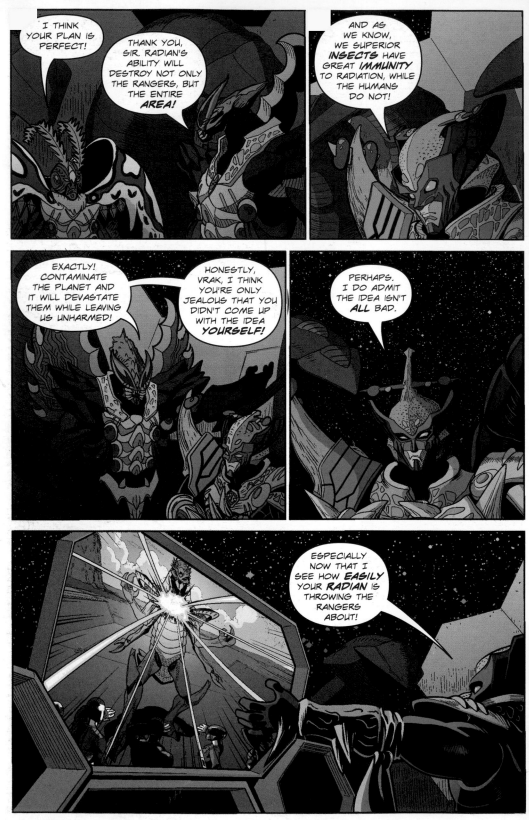

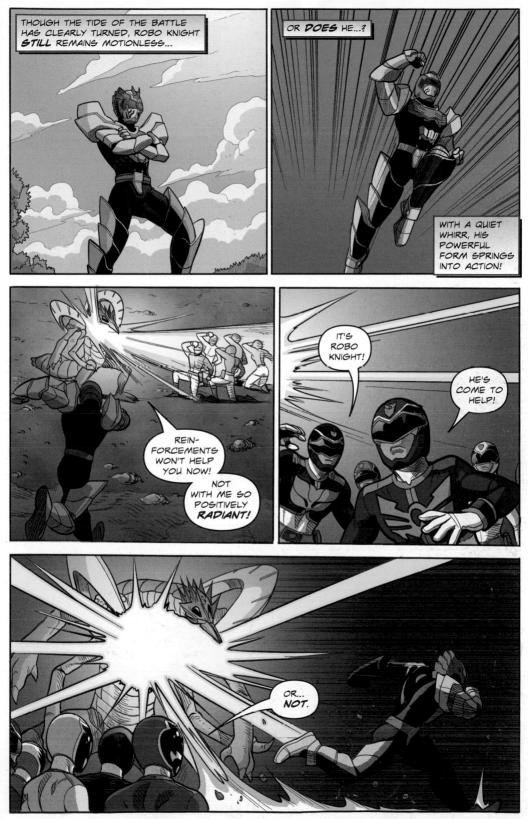

THOUGH THE TIDE OF THE BATTLE HAS CLEARLY TURNED, ROBO KNIGHT **STILL** REMAINS MOTIONLESS...

OR **DOES** HE...?

WITH A QUIET WHIRR, HIS POWERFUL FORM SPRINGS INTO ACTION!

REIN-FORCEMENTS WON'T HELP YOU NOW! NOT WITH ME SO POSITIVELY **RADIANT!**

IT'S ROBO KNIGHT!

HE'S COME TO HELP!

OR... NOT.

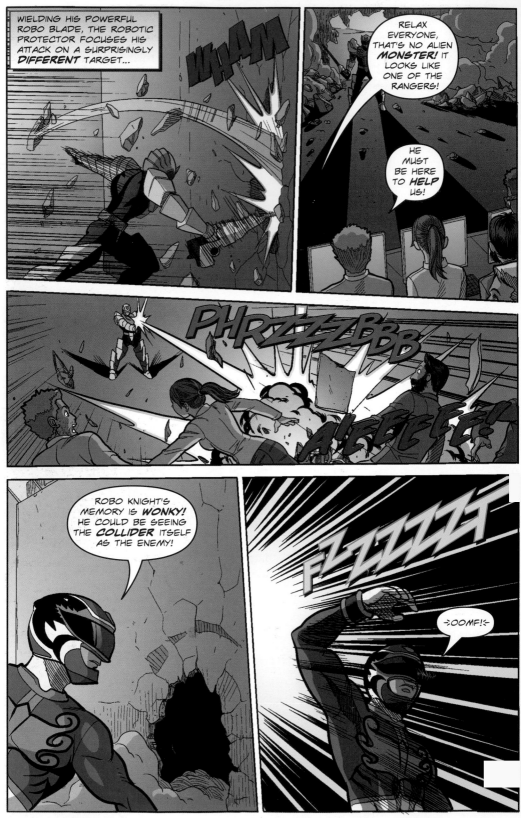

WIELDING HIS POWERFUL ROBO BLADE, THE ROBOTIC PROTECTOR FOCUSES HIS ATTACK ON A SURPRISINGLY **DIFFERENT** TARGET...

WHAM

RELAX EVERYONE, THAT'S NO ALIEN **MONSTER!** IT LOOKS LIKE ONE OF THE RANGERS!

HE **MUST** BE HERE TO **HELP** US!

PHRZZZBBB

AIEEEEE!

ROBO KNIGHT'S MEMORY IS **WONKY!** HE COULD BE SEEING THE **COLLIDER** ITSELF AS THE ENEMY!

FZZZZZT

≥OOMF!≤

33

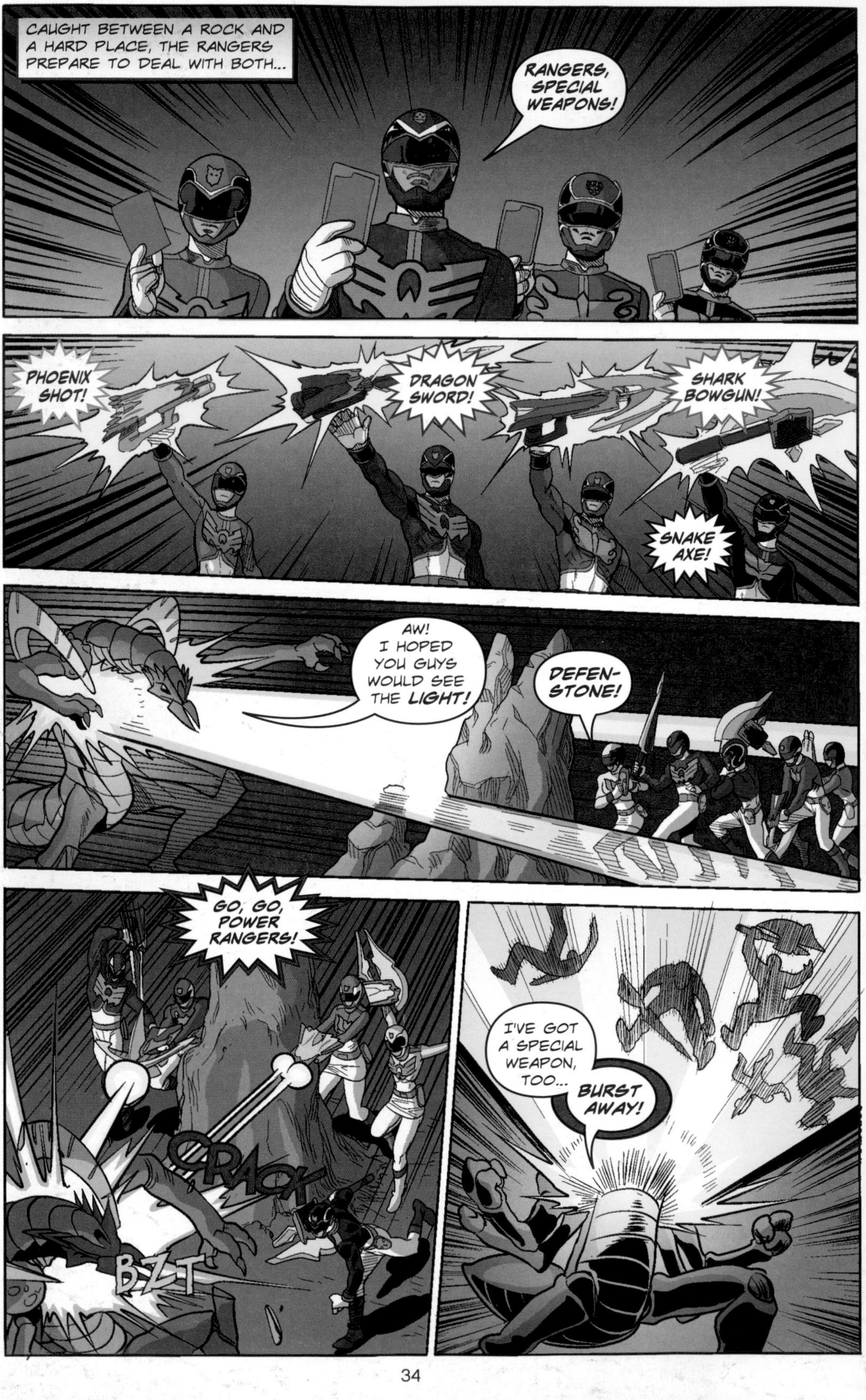
CAUGHT BETWEEN A ROCK AND A HARD PLACE, THE RANGERS PREPARE TO DEAL WITH BOTH...
RANGERS, SPECIAL WEAPONS!
PHOENIX SHOT!
DRAGON SWORD!
SHARK BOWGUN!
SNAKE AXE!
AW! I HOPED YOU GUYS WOULD SEE THE LIGHT!
DEFEN-STONE!
GO, GO, POWER RANGERS!
CRACK
BZZT
I'VE GOT A SPECIAL WEAPON, TOO... BURST AWAY!

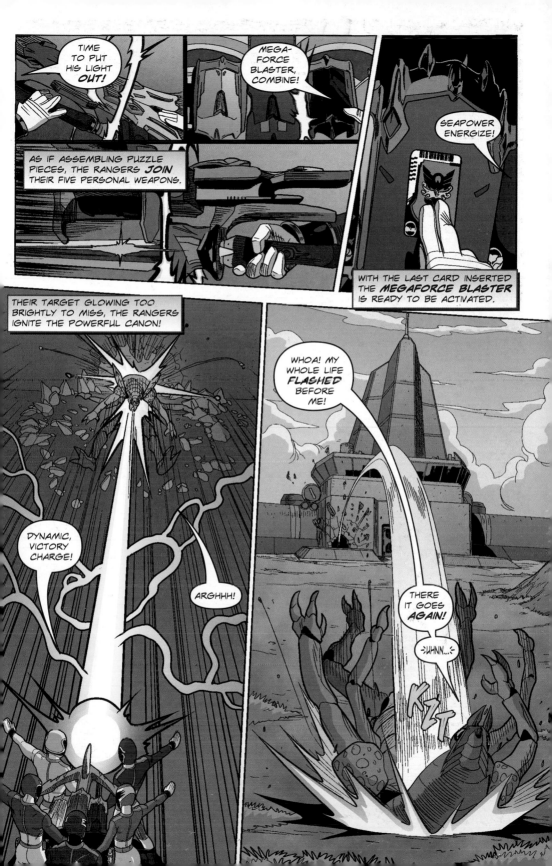

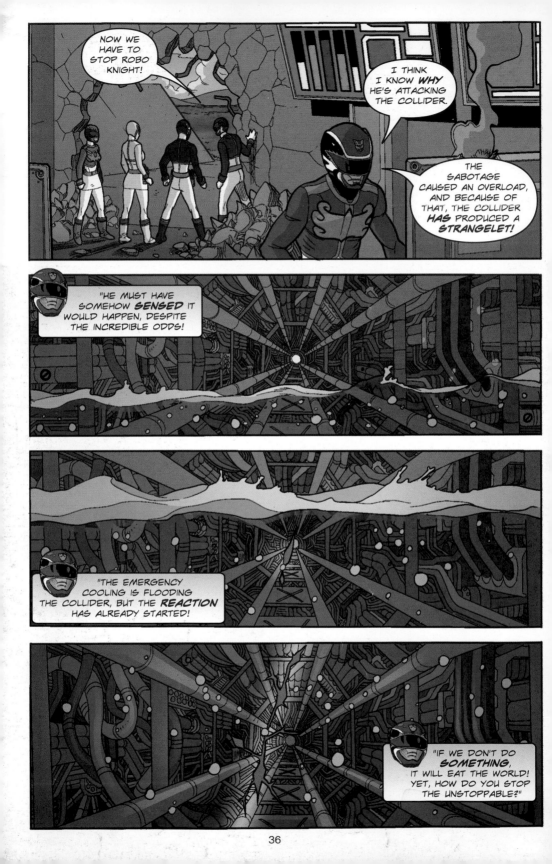

NOW WE HAVE TO STOP ROBO KNIGHT!

I THINK I KNOW **WHY** HE'S ATTACKING THE COLLIDER.

THE SABOTAGE CAUSED AN OVERLOAD, AND BECAUSE OF THAT, THE COLLIDER **HAS** PRODUCED A **STRANGELET!**

"HE MUST HAVE SOMEHOW **SENSED** IT WOULD HAPPEN, DESPITE THE INCREDIBLE ODDS!"

"THE EMERGENCY COOLING IS FLOODING THE COLLIDER, BUT THE **REACTION** HAS ALREADY STARTED!"

"IF WE DON'T DO **SOMETHING**, IT WILL EAT THE WORLD! YET, HOW DO YOU STOP THE UNSTOPPABLE?"

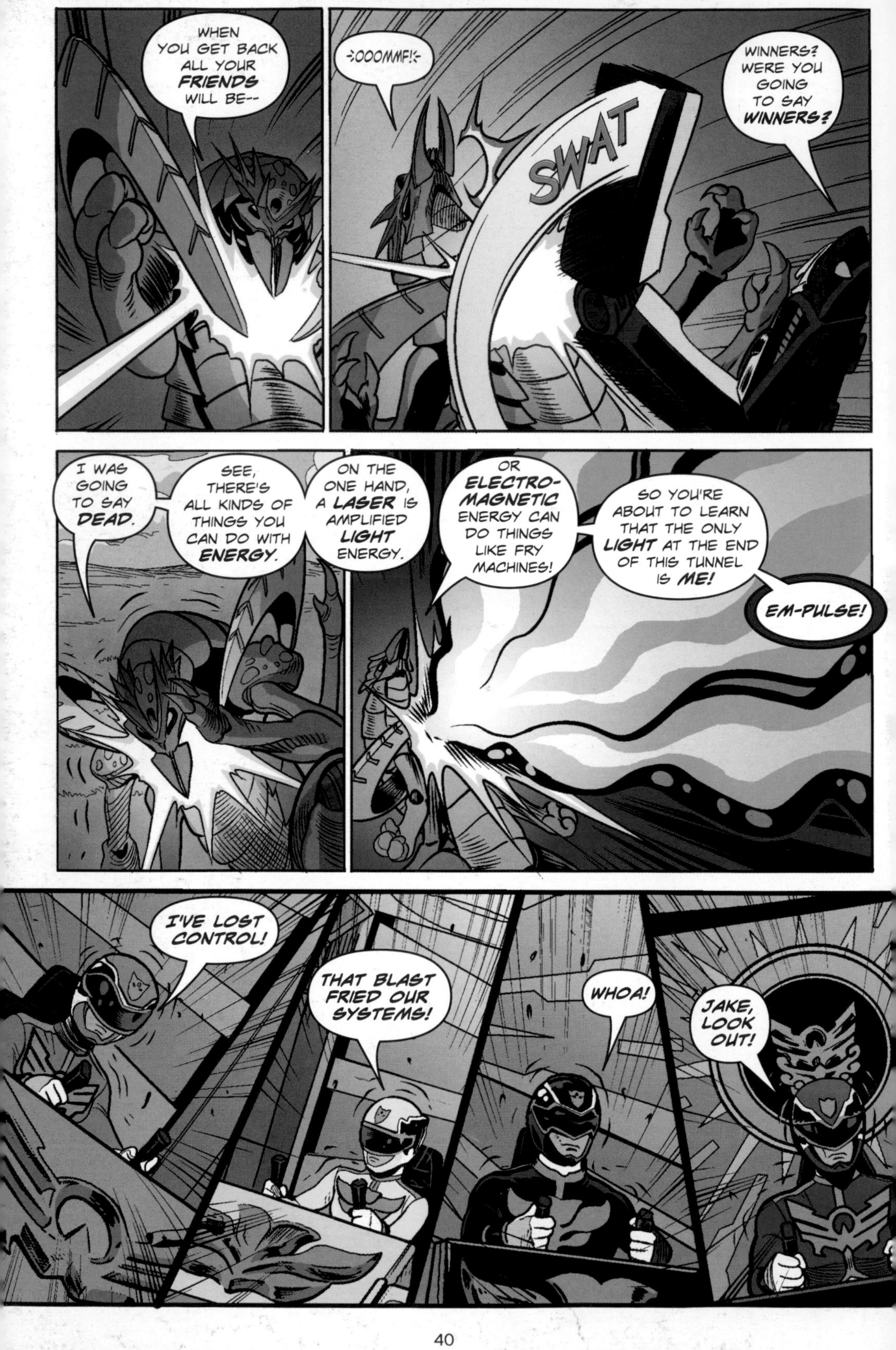

WHEN YOU GET BACK ALL YOUR FRIENDS WILL BE--
-:OOOMMF!:-
SWAT
WINNERS? WERE YOU GOING TO SAY WINNERS?
I WAS GOING TO SAY DEAD.
SEE, THERE'S ALL KINDS OF THINGS YOU CAN DO WITH ENERGY.
ON THE ONE HAND, A LASER IS AMPLIFIED LIGHT ENERGY.
OR ELECTRO-MAGNETIC ENERGY CAN DO THINGS LIKE FRY MACHINES!
SO YOU'RE ABOUT TO LEARN THAT THE ONLY LIGHT AT THE END OF THIS TUNNEL IS ME!
EM-PULSE!
I'VE LOST CONTROL!
THAT BLAST FRIED OUR SYSTEMS!
WHOA!
JAKE, LOOK OUT!

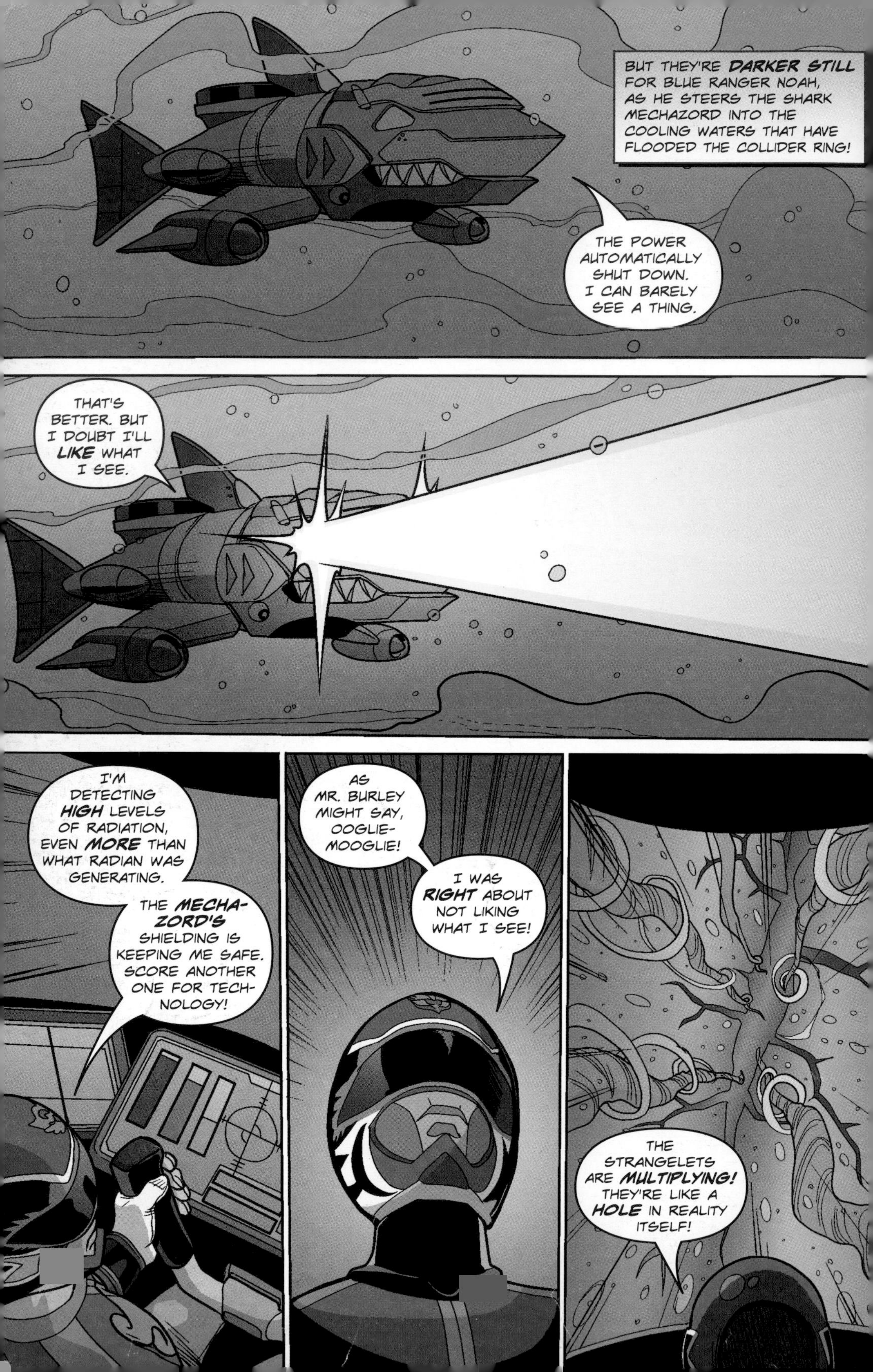

BUT THEY'RE DARKER STILL FOR BLUE RANGER NOAH, AS HE STEERS THE SHARK MECHAZORD INTO THE COOLING WATERS THAT HAVE FLOODED THE COLLIDER RING!
THE POWER AUTOMATICALLY SHUT DOWN. I CAN BARELY SEE A THING.
THAT'S BETTER. BUT I DOUBT I'LL LIKE WHAT I SEE.
I'M DETECTING HIGH LEVELS OF RADIATION, EVEN MORE THAN WHAT RADIAN WAS GENERATING.
THE MECHA-ZORD'S SHIELDING IS KEEPING ME SAFE. SCORE ANOTHER ONE FOR TECH-NOLOGY!
AS MR. BURLEY MIGHT SAY, OOGLIE-MOOGLIE!
I WAS RIGHT ABOUT NOT LIKING WHAT I SEE!
THE STRANGELETS ARE MULTIPLYING! THEY'RE LIKE A HOLE IN REALITY ITSELF!

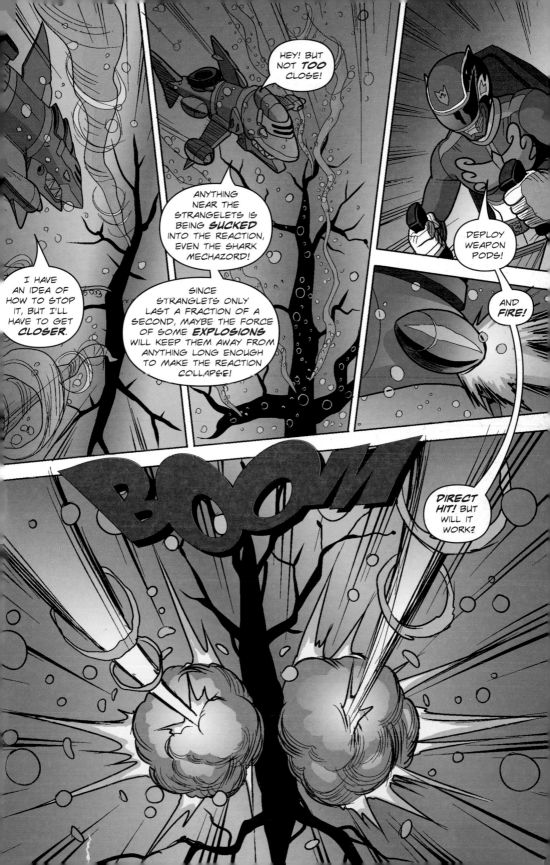

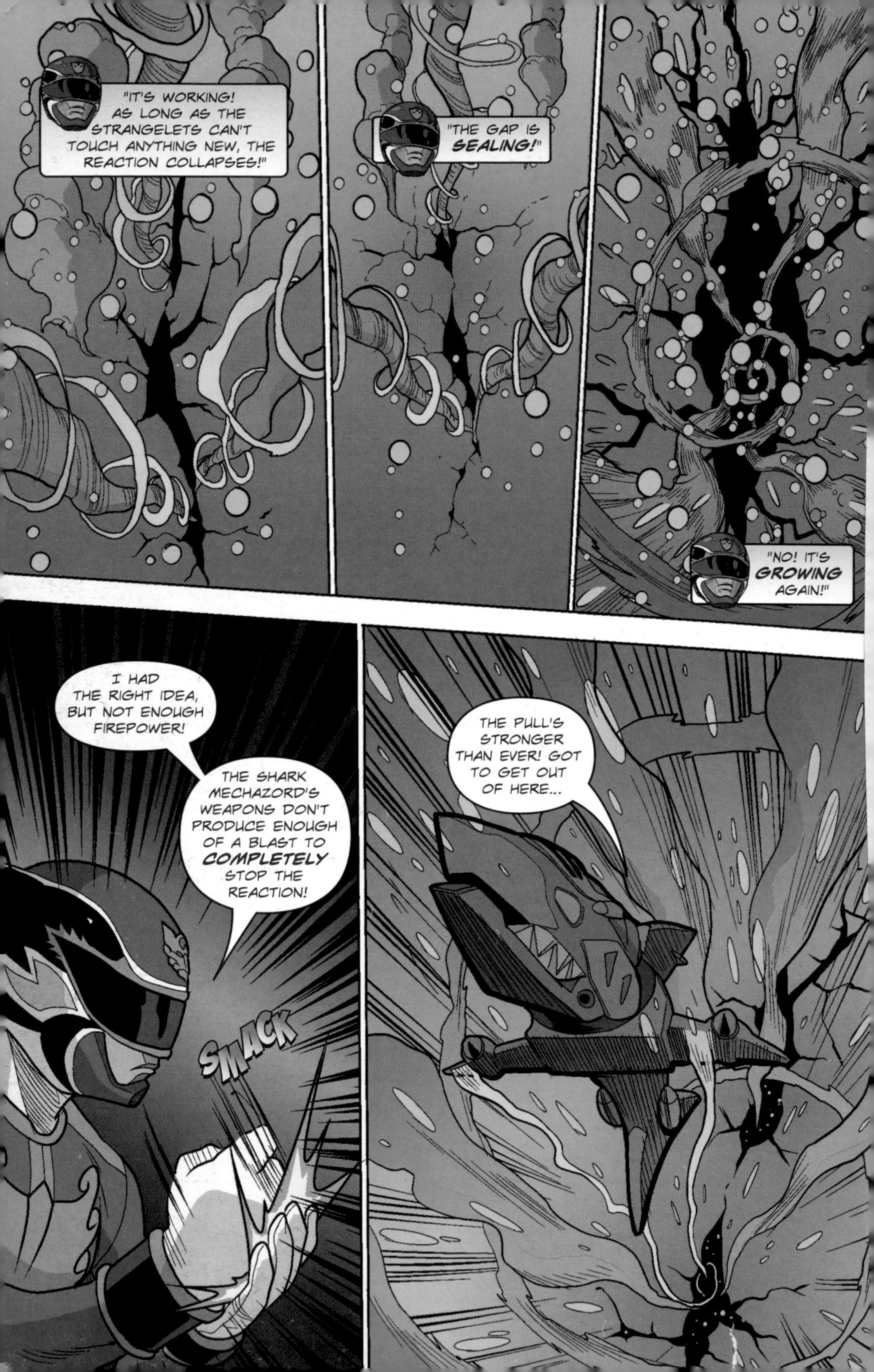

"IT'S WORKING! AS LONG AS THE STRANGELETS CAN'T TOUCH ANYTHING NEW, THE REACTION COLLAPSES!"
"THE GAP IS SEALING!"
"NO! IT'S GROWING AGAIN!"
I HAD THE RIGHT IDEA, BUT NOT ENOUGH FIREPOWER!
THE SHARK MECHAZORD'S WEAPONS DON'T PRODUCE ENOUGH OF A BLAST TO COMPLETELY STOP THE REACTION!
SMACK
THE PULL'S STRONGER THAN EVER! GOT TO GET OUT OF HERE...

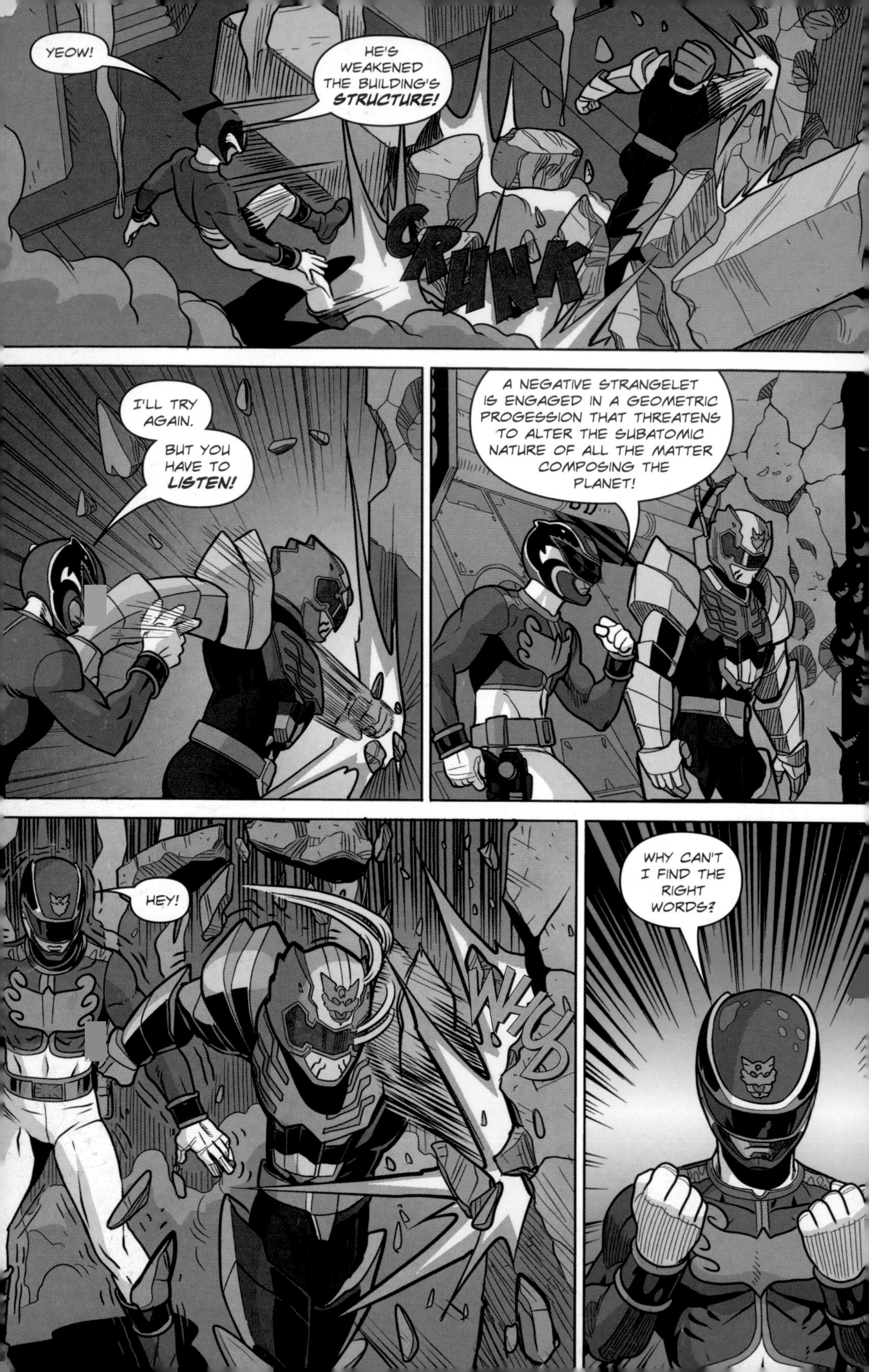
YEOW!
HE'S WEAKENED THE BUILDING'S STRUCTURE!
CRUNK
I'LL TRY AGAIN.
BUT YOU HAVE TO LISTEN!
A NEGATIVE STRANGELET IS ENGAGED IN A GEOMETRIC PROGESSION THAT THREATENS TO ALTER THE SUBATOMIC NATURE OF ALL THE MATTER COMPOSING THE PLANET!
HEY!
WHUD
WHY CAN'T I FIND THE RIGHT WORDS?

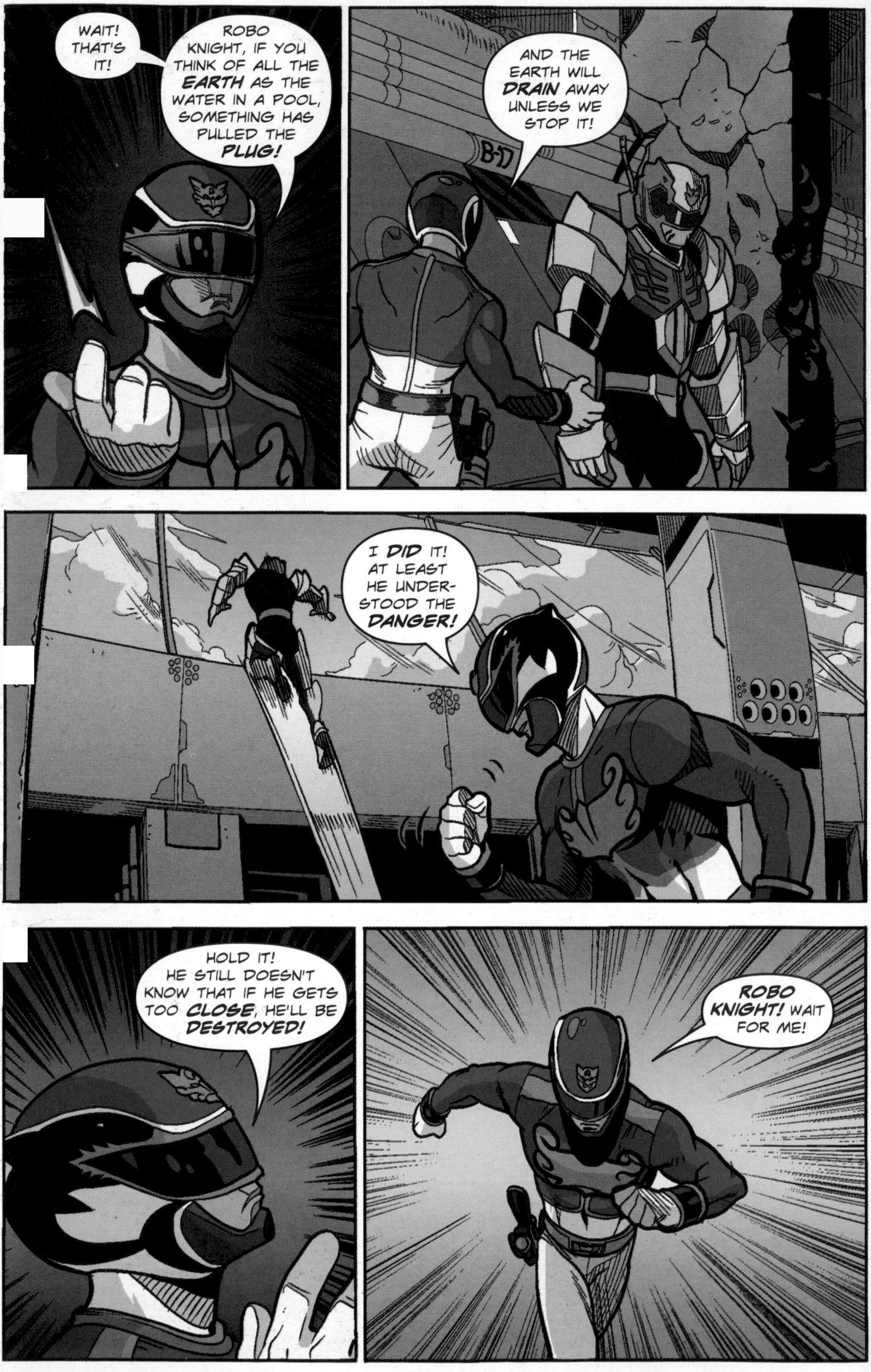
WAIT! THAT'S IT!
ROBO KNIGHT, IF YOU THINK OF ALL THE EARTH AS THE WATER IN A POOL, SOMETHING HAS PULLED THE PLUG!
AND THE EARTH WILL DRAIN AWAY UNLESS WE STOP IT!
B-17
I DID IT! AT LEAST HE UNDER-STOOD THE DANGER!
HOLD IT! HE STILL DOESN'T KNOW THAT IF HE GETS TOO CLOSE, HE'LL BE DESTROYED!
ROBO KNIGHT! WAIT FOR ME!

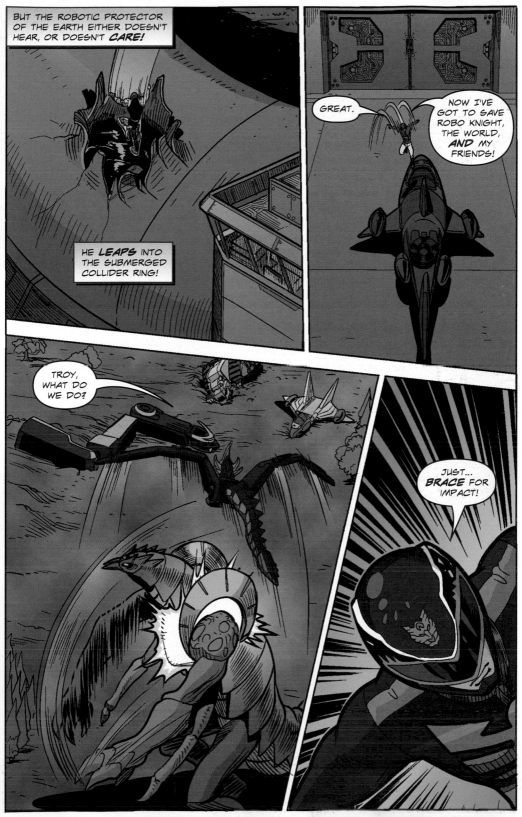

BUT THE ROBOTIC PROTECTOR OF THE EARTH EITHER DOESN'T HEAR, OR DOESN'T **CARE!**

HE **LEAPS** INTO THE SUBMERGED COLLIDER RING!

GREAT.

NOW I'VE GOT TO SAVE ROBO KNIGHT, THE WORLD, **AND** MY FRIENDS!

TROY, WHAT DO WE DO?

JUST... **BRACE** FOR IMPACT!

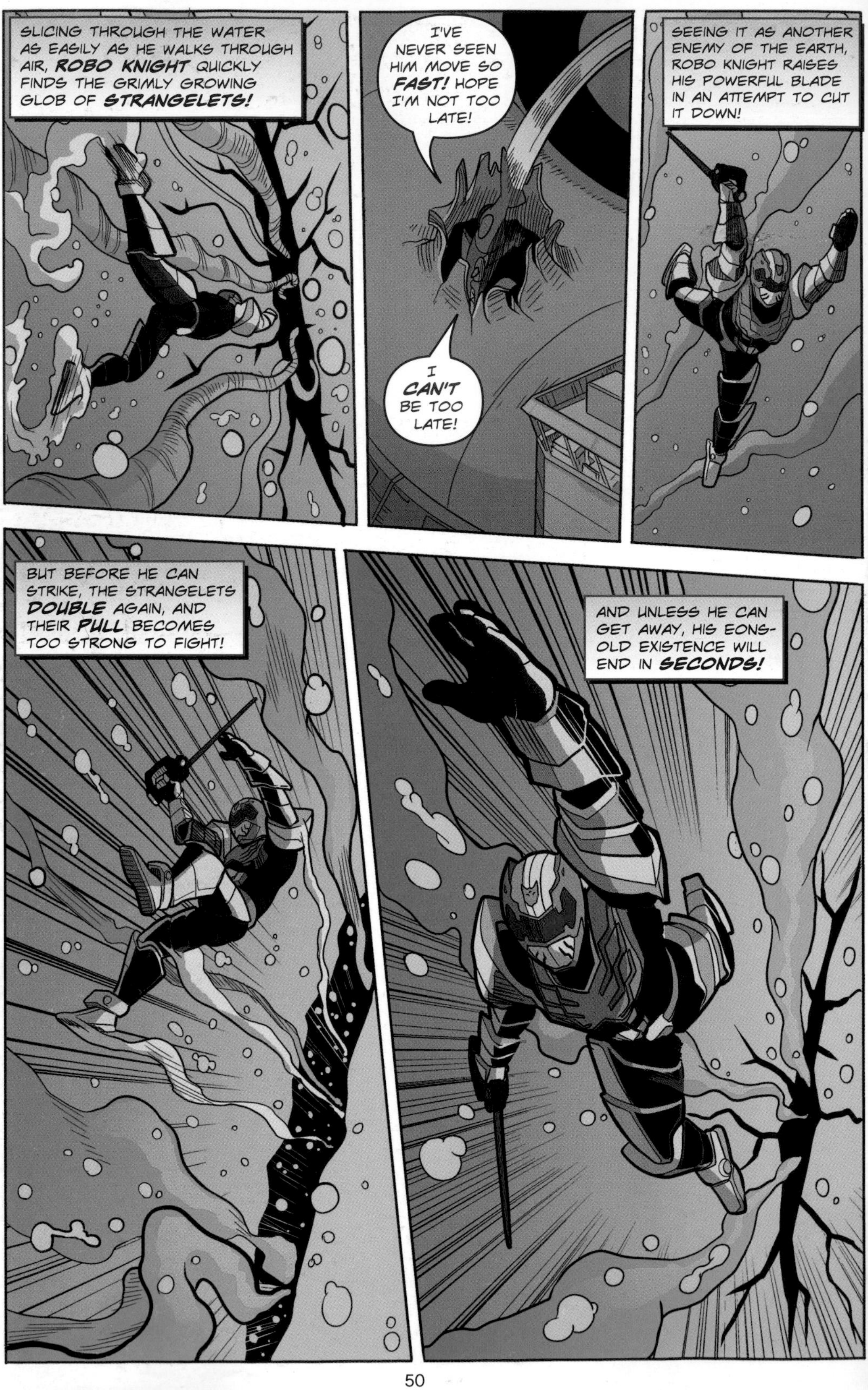
SLICING THROUGH THE WATER AS EASILY AS HE WALKS THROUGH AIR, ROBO KNIGHT QUICKLY FINDS THE GRIMLY GROWING GLOB OF STRANGELETS!
I'VE NEVER SEEN HIM MOVE SO FAST! HOPE I'M NOT TOO LATE!
I CAN'T BE TOO LATE!
SEEING IT AS ANOTHER ENEMY OF THE EARTH, ROBO KNIGHT RAISES HIS POWERFUL BLADE IN AN ATTEMPT TO CUT IT DOWN!
BUT BEFORE HE CAN STRIKE, THE STRANGELETS DOUBLE AGAIN, AND THEIR PULL BECOMES TOO STRONG TO FIGHT!
AND UNLESS HE CAN GET AWAY, HIS EONS-OLD EXISTENCE WILL END IN SECONDS!

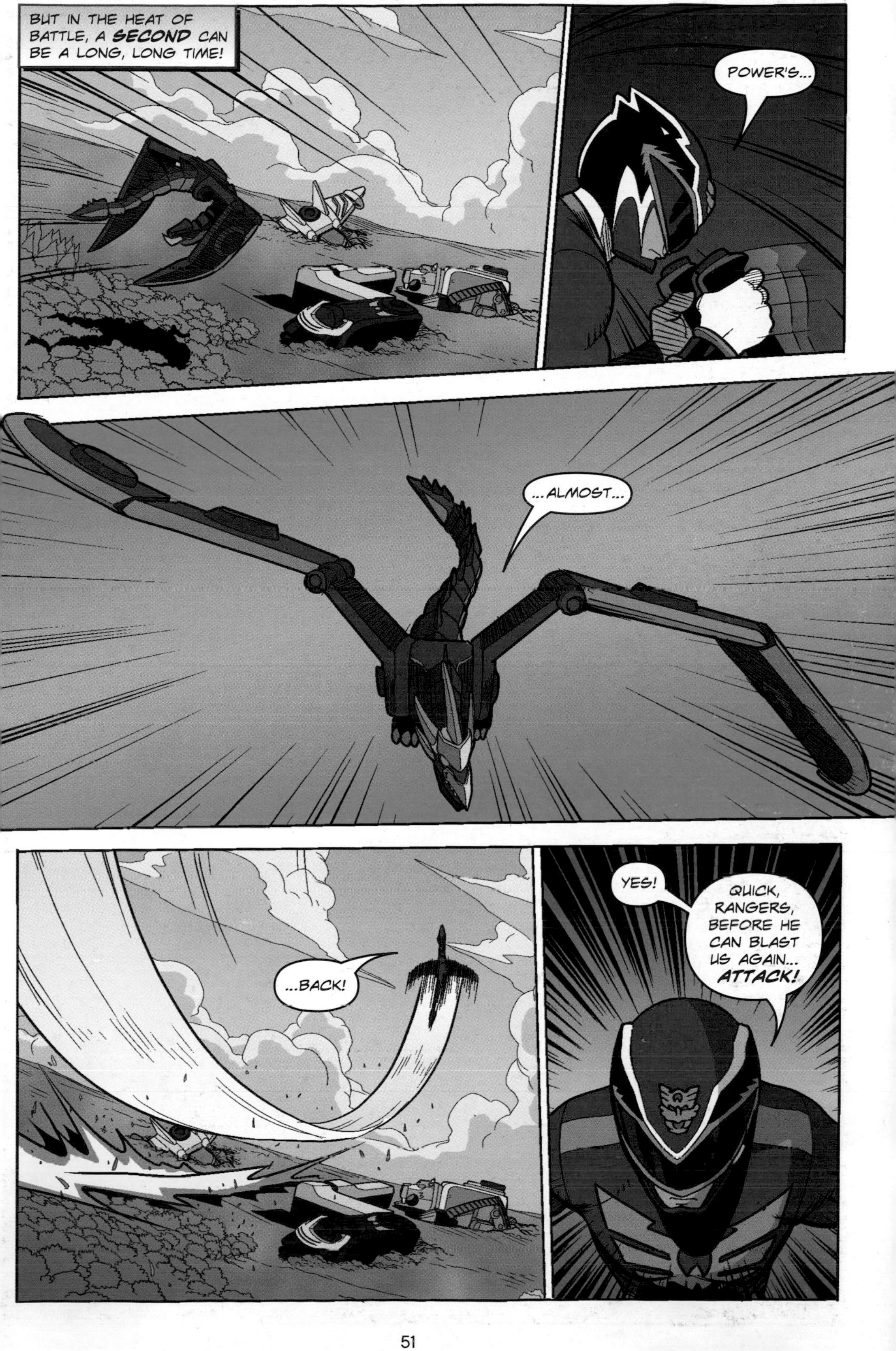
BUT IN THE HEAT OF BATTLE, A SECOND CAN BE A LONG, LONG TIME!
POWER'S...
...ALMOST...
...BACK!
YES!
QUICK, RANGERS, BEFORE HE CAN BLAST US AGAIN... ATTACK!

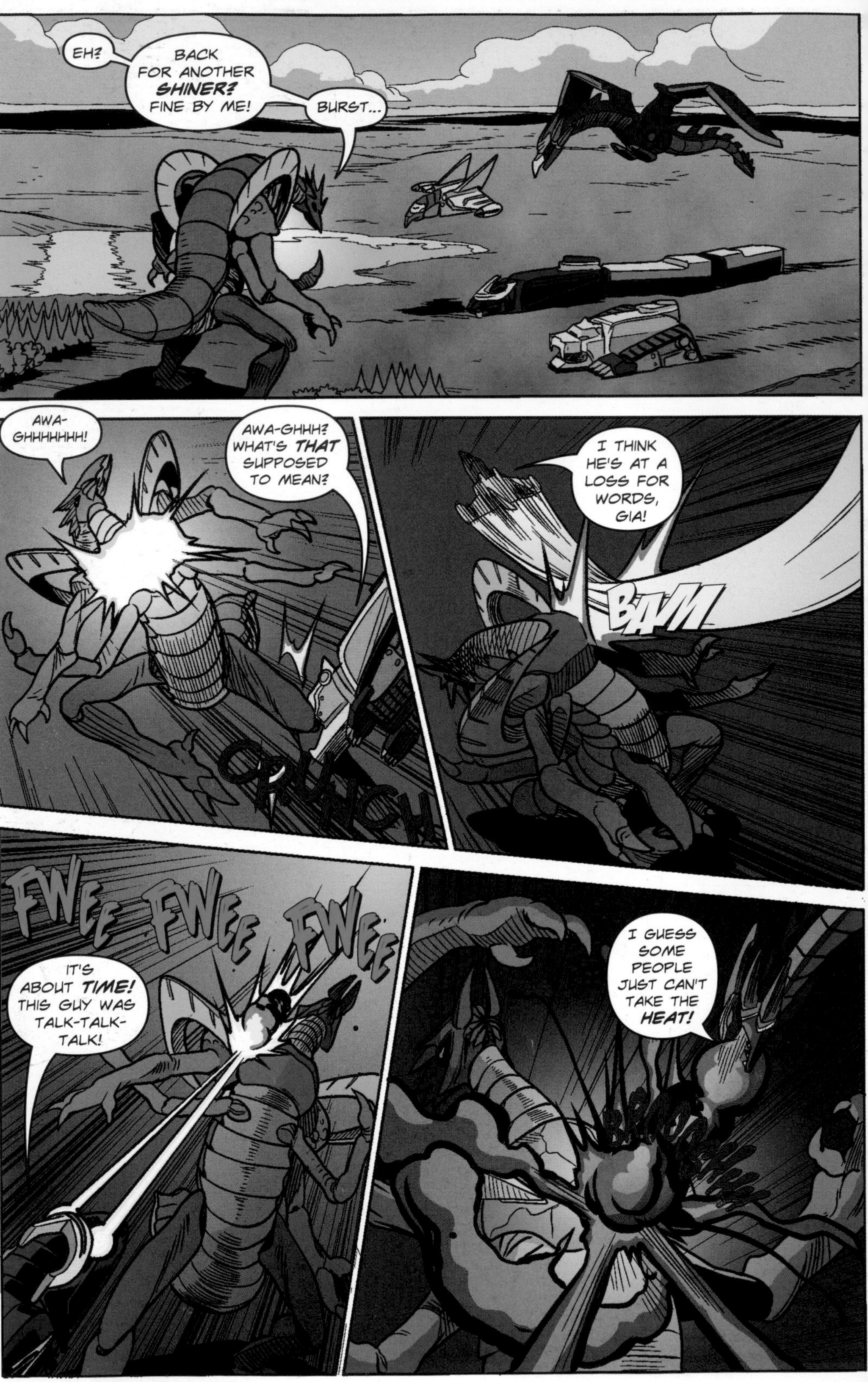
EH?
BACK FOR ANOTHER **SHINER?** FINE BY ME!
BURST...
AWA-GHHHHHHH!
AWA-GHHH? WHAT'S **THAT** SUPPOSED TO MEAN?
CRUNCH
I THINK HE'S AT A LOSS FOR WORDS, GIA!
BAM
FWEE FWEE FWEE
IT'S ABOUT **TIME!** THIS GUY WAS TALK-TALK-TALK!
I GUESS SOME PEOPLE JUST CAN'T TAKE THE **HEAT!**

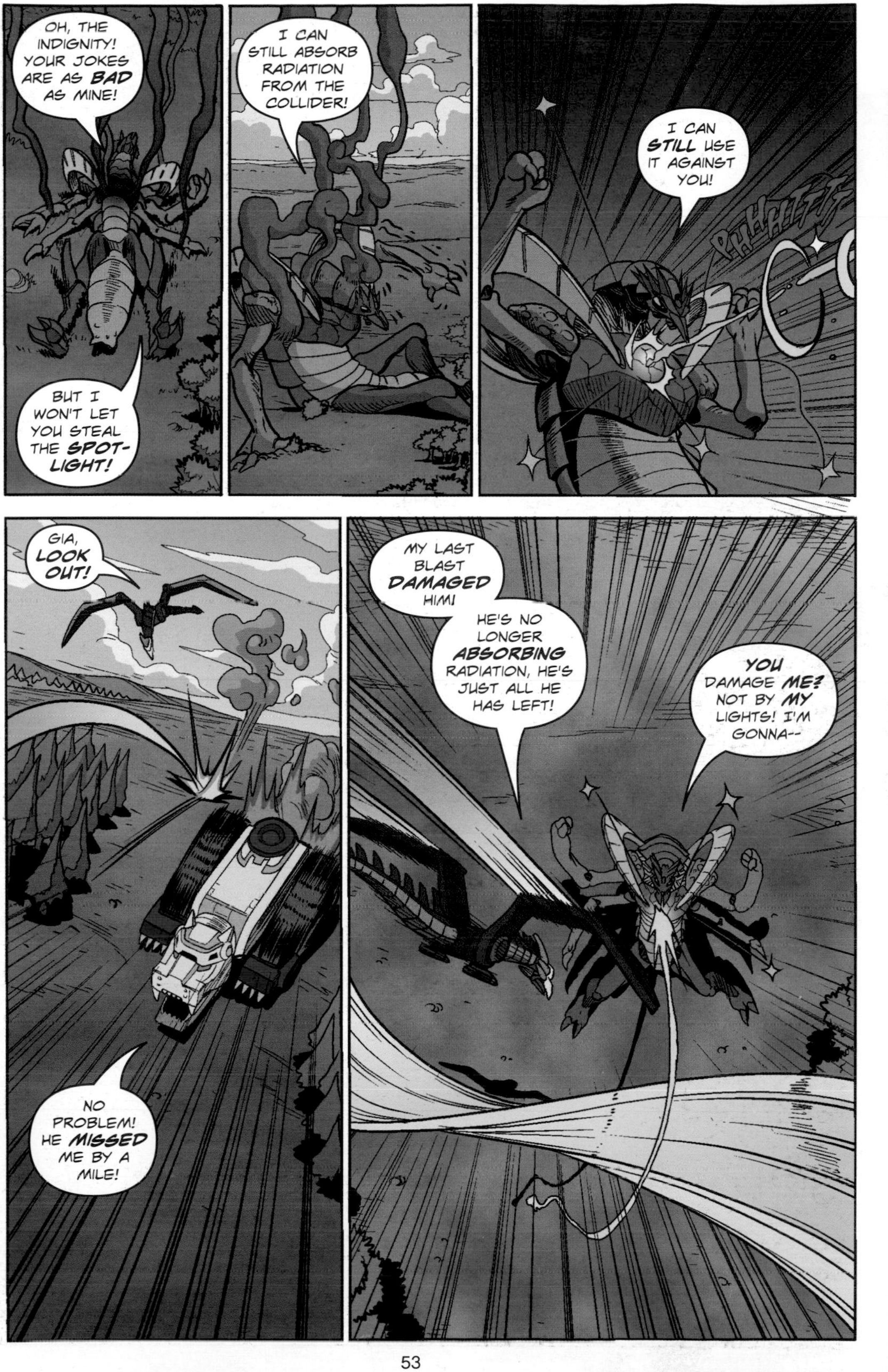
OH, THE INDIGNITY! YOUR JOKES ARE AS **BAD** AS MINE!
BUT I WON'T LET YOU STEAL THE **SPOT-LIGHT!**
I CAN STILL ABSORB RADIATION FROM THE COLLIDER!
I CAN **STILL** USE IT AGAINST YOU!
PHHHTTT
GIA, **LOOK OUT!**
NO PROBLEM! HE **MISSED** ME BY A MILE!
MY LAST BLAST **DAMAGED** HIM!
HE'S NO LONGER **ABSORBING** RADIATION, HE'S JUST ALL HE HAS LEFT!
YOU DAMAGE **ME?** NOT BY **MY** LIGHTS! I'M GONNA--

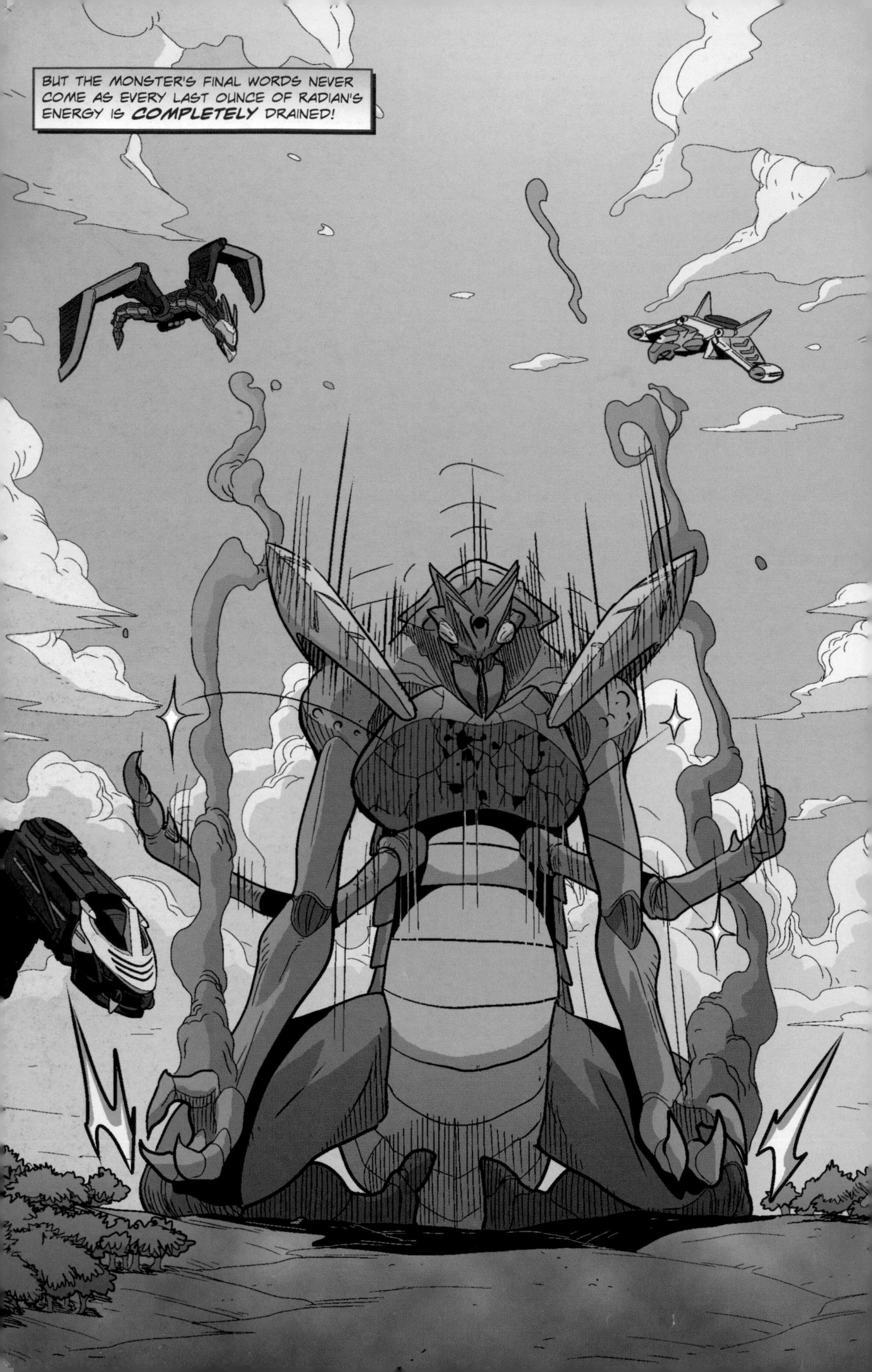
BUT THE MONSTER'S FINAL WORDS NEVER COME AS EVERY LAST OUNCE OF RADIAN'S ENERGY IS COMPLETELY DRAINED!

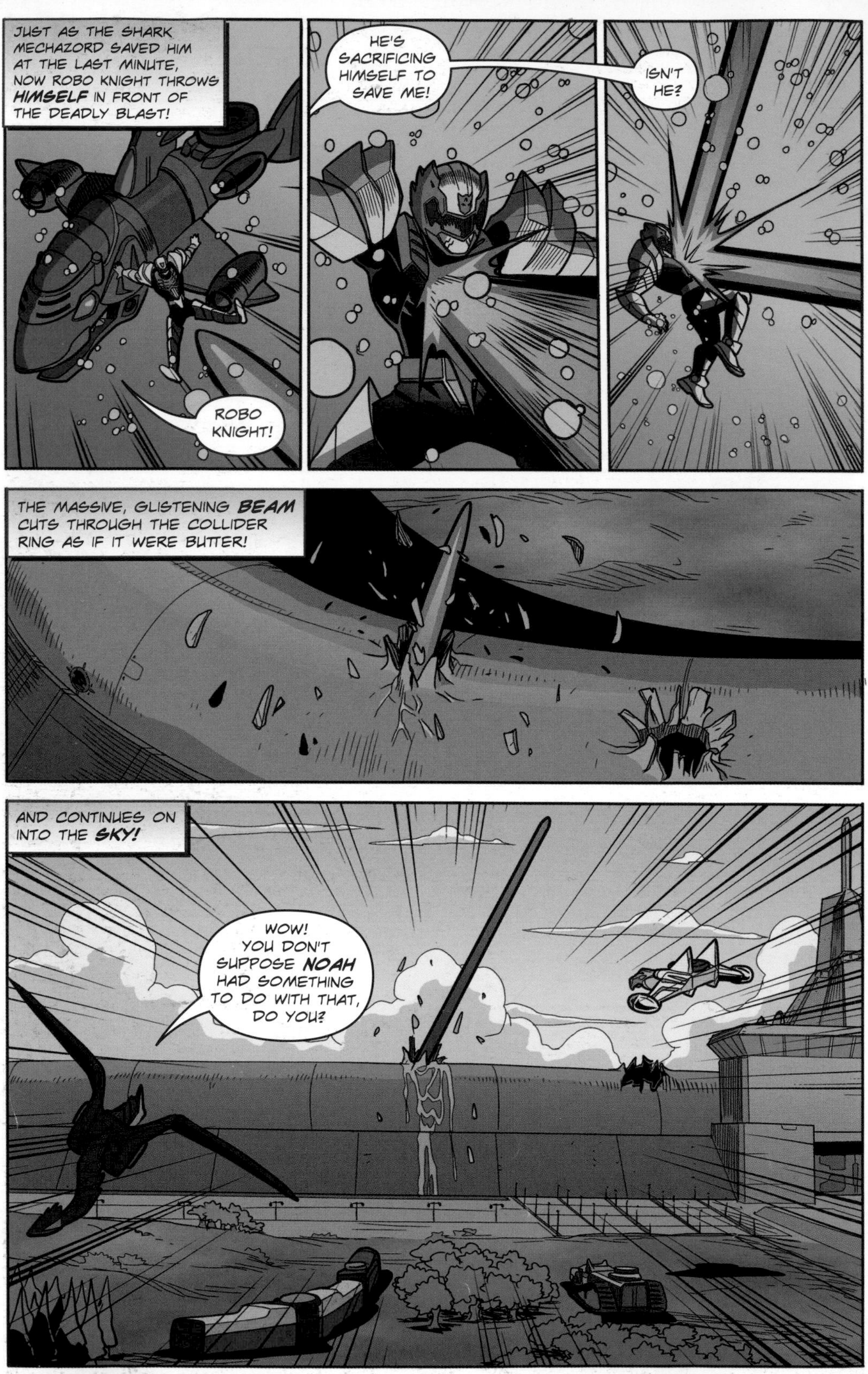
JUST AS THE SHARK MECHAZORD SAVED HIM AT THE LAST MINUTE, NOW ROBO KNIGHT THROWS HIMSELF IN FRONT OF THE DEADLY BLAST!
ROBO KNIGHT!
HE'S SACRIFICING HIMSELF TO SAVE ME!
ISN'T HE?
THE MASSIVE, GLISTENING BEAM CUTS THROUGH THE COLLIDER RING AS IF IT WERE BUTTER!
AND CONTINUES ON INTO THE SKY!
WOW! YOU DON'T SUPPOSE NOAH HAD SOMETHING TO DO WITH THAT, DO YOU?

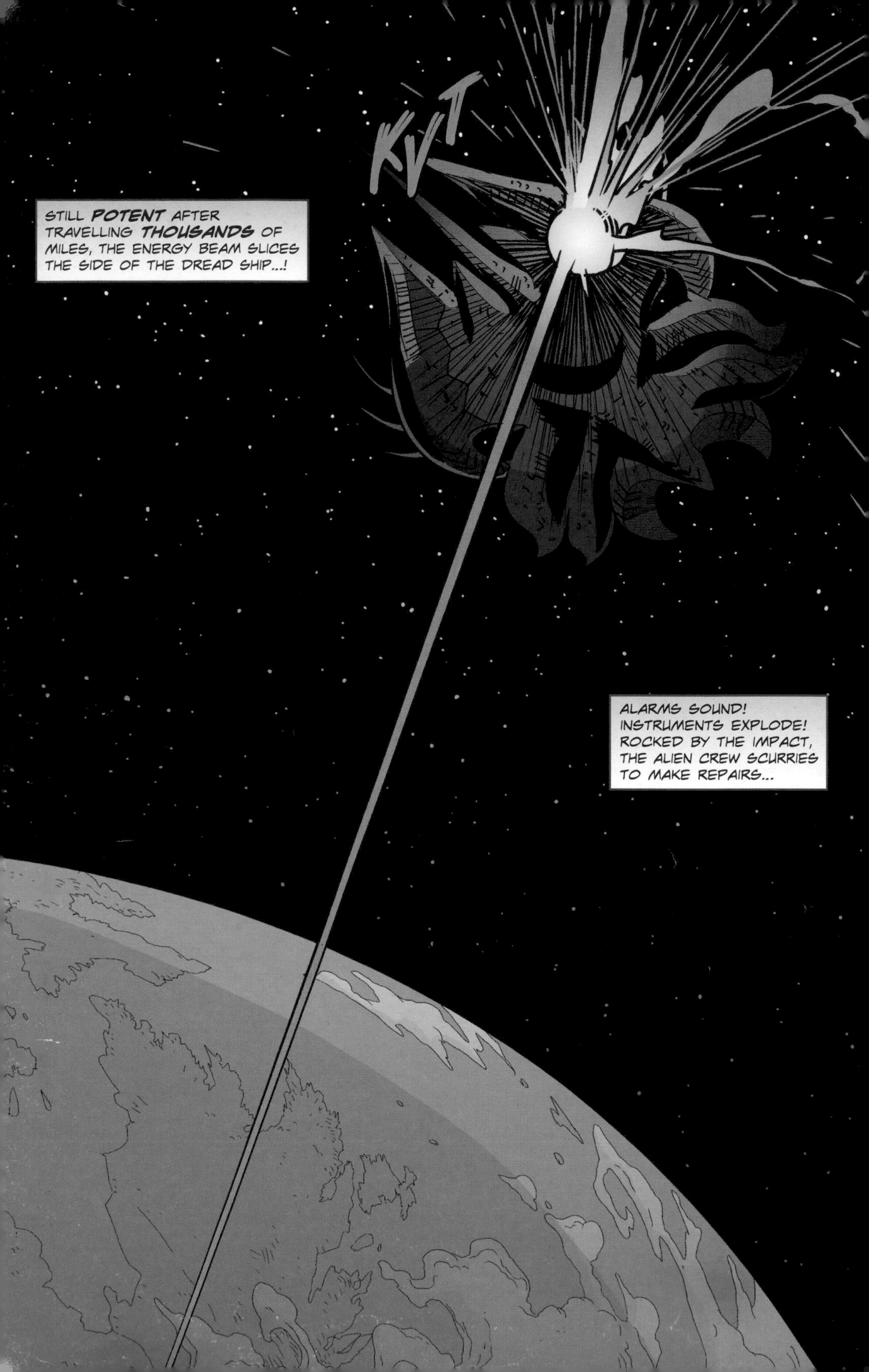
KVT
STILL POTENT AFTER TRAVELLING THOUSANDS OF MILES, THE ENERGY BEAM SLICES THE SIDE OF THE DREAD SHIP...!
ALARMS SOUND! INSTRUMENTS EXPLODE! ROCKED BY THE IMPACT, THE ALIEN CREW SCURRIES TO MAKE REPAIRS...

AS THE WARSTAR SHIP STRUGGLES, BACK ON EARTH...

IT'S NOAH!

THAT WAS **CLOSE! REAL** CLOSE!

BUT YOU'RE **ALL RIGHT**, AND THE WORLD IS **STILL** HERE!

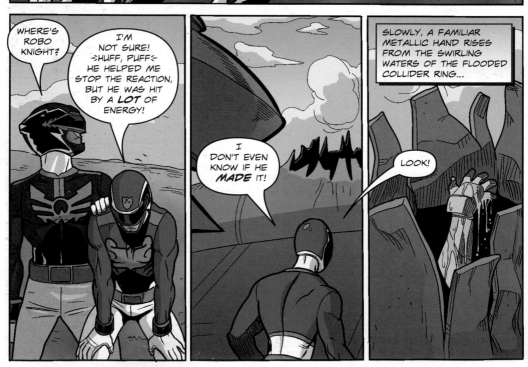

WHERE'S ROBO KNIGHT?

I'M NOT SURE! ⇒HUFF, PUFF⇐ HE HELPED ME STOP THE REACTION, BUT HE WAS HIT BY A **LOT** OF ENERGY!

I DON'T EVEN KNOW IF HE **MADE** IT!

SLOWLY, A FAMILIAR METALLIC HAND RISES FROM THE SWIRLING WATERS OF THE FLOODED COLLIDER RING...

LOOK!